I0761925

That's what happened when a person lived thirty minutes out of town.

You had no friends. And if you did have friends, they weren't going to spend half a day driving out to feed a cat everyday.

For an entire month.

Out of options, I'd driven here from Atlanta just to get the cat.

Just because I didn't want to be here was no reason for the cat to starve while Grandpa was in rehab.

I needed to try to see Grandpa, but what I really needed to do was to get back to Atlanta.

So I had a couple of other things to do, then I was going to throw the cat in his carrier and head out of here.

I had my reasons for not wanting to be here at the Becquerel estate. It had nothing to do with my family. Nothing to do with Grandpa.

And it had everything to do with an experience I'd had when I was just fifteen years old.

An experience I'd had in the mist.

I'd never told a single soul.

But I'd never forgotten it.

And never would.

PROMISED IN THE MIST

ALSO BY KATHRYN KALEIGH

THE BECQUERELS

Twist of Fate

When the Stars Align

Once in a Blue Moon

Once Upon a Christmas

A Wish Upon a Star

Written in the Wind

Scripted in the Stars

Destined in the Twilight

Promised in the Mist

Trapped in the Melody

When Lightning Strikes

Storm of Time

Midnight Storm

When the Moon Falls

Stormborn Angel

Time Tempest

The Heart Remembers

A Moment in Time

Moonlight Shadows

Rescued in Time

PROMISED IN THE MIST

THE BECQUERELS

INTO THE MIST

KATHRYN KALEIGH

PROMISED IN THE MIST

PREVIEW: TRAPPED IN THE MELODY

Written by Kathryn Kaleigh

Published by KST Publishing, Inc., 2022

Cover by Skyhouse24Media

www.kathrynkaleigh.com

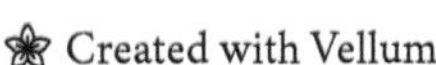

To learn more about Kathryn Kaleigh, visit

www.kathrynkaleigh.com

Kathryn Kaleigh

PROLOGUE

It was a given that a fifteen-year-old boy left to his own devices in the country would get into trouble.

Grant Laurent was no exception.

Today it was hot as the devil, so he had done what any reasonable teen would do. He had gone down to the murky, smelly Mississippi River bank to hunt frogs.

He'd been successful, too. He had a big son-of-a-bitching bull frog in his burlap bag. It kicked and squeaked, but he'd let it out soon enough. He wasn't cruel. He had good plans for it, though, before he set it free.

Hell, his cousins would probably want to eat it. Northerners—and yes, Natchez was the north compared to New Orleans—were strange people.

Walking along the road leading away from the river toward the house, he slung the sack over his shoulder and whistled a nonsensible tune.

He was the only one outside. Everyone else was inside, avoiding the hottest part of the sunny day. But not Grant. Grant was a man with a purpose. And today's purpose was to send his sister squealing.

A flock of blue birds fluttered from one of the old oak trees, taking flight into the cloudless sky.

That was definitely one of the benefits—few as they were—to spending summers up here in the country. There was far more to get into.

His parents packed up the whole family and traveled here every year for the three or four hottest months of the summer.

Mother was deathly afraid of contracting the yellow fever. Father's parents had both died from it before Grant was even born, but it left a lasting impression on Mother.

Following the bend in the road, he could see the house up ahead. A huge three-story house with tall white columns from ground to roof. He personally preferred his town home in New Orleans with the courtyard right in the middle, but this was the style out here in the country.

A cool breeze swept through the trees, sending the moss flying like silver flags on a pirate ship.

He shivered. This was full on June. There should be no cool spells. Maybe a little cool in the mornings, but that burned off quick enough.

There were some dark clouds banking in the southwest. If they were in New Orleans, he'd say there was a hurricane coming in. But they were much too far inland for that.

He shrugged it off and kept walking.

It made no difference to him. He had his frog and he was happy.

As he rounded another bend, he noticed that there was a layer of mist coming in. The kind of mist that sometimes lingered over the Mississippi River early in the mornings.

Now that was weird.

He stopped and looked behind him, but the mist was everywhere. And he was alone.

He took another step, but something invisible seemed to push back, keeping him from going any further.

He would have expected something like this in New Orleans, but it was the first time he'd encountered anything other than the mundane up here.

Intrigued, but like most fifteen-year-old boys, not afraid of anything, he turned around again to see what he could see behind him.

He couldn't see anything other than the mist, but it was what he didn't see… didn't hear… that was most interesting.

He didn't hear anything at all. No steamboat whistle. No dogs braying at squirrels. No birds.

He slowly turned back around, ready to get on to the house now.

Enough was enough already.

His feet froze to the ground, this time of their own accord.

A girl, about his age, stood not more than three feet in front of him.

The wind whipped at her long black hair. She stood perfectly still, not bothering to sweep it out of her eyes.

She was wearing nothing but a pair of short blue pants that left her legs scandalously bear all the way down to a pair of white shoes. Her top was equally risqué. A tight light blue material that left her arms bare. The scooped neck accented her bosom.

He took in all of this with a split-second glance, but it was her eyes that enchanted him.

Big green eyes framed with thick dark lashes. Her skin was white as snow and her lips red and plush.

She was frowning at him from that beautiful face.

He just grinned in response. Confronted with such beauty looking at him with adorable consternation, there was nothing else he could do.

The mist swirled at their feet, but they were alone in a cocoon of silence.

Then the wind stopped blowing her hair. It just stopped.

The moss in the trees around us still blew in the wind, but within their little bubble, there was no sound. No wind. Nothing but mist swirling at their feet.

They tried again to take a step forward. Managed one step.

He swallowed the emotion that overwhelmed him and took another step forward.

If she was really there, he wanted to touch her. To feel her.

She, too, took a step forward and now they were standing merely inches apart.

She looked up at me with her beautiful green eyes, framed with long thick lashes, her mouth parted ever so slightly. Her breathing was shallow as though she had just run a long distance. And he felt much the same way.

"I can't…" He held up a hand, palm out, unable to get his thoughts formed into words. "Are you real?"

She held her own hand up, her palm facing, but not touching, his.

"I'm real," she said.

They stood there with our hands held up as though they stood on two sides of a window, able to see each other, but unable to actually touch.

But it wasn't enough. Would never be enough.

He wanted to actually touch her.

To know that she was real.

"As am I," he said, searching her eyes.

Then unable to stop himself, he pressed his hand forward, clasping her fingers in his.

She was real. She was so very real.

Now that he had touched her, he couldn't get enough.

He lifted his other hand, with every intent of taking her other hand, too, but that did not happen.

She began to fade.

Her fingers slipped out of his. He leaned forward, trying to keep his grip on her.

But the girl quite simply faded away.

The mist receded along with the wind and the cool breeze. A steamboat blew its familiar horn on the river behind him and a dog brayed.

His burlap sack had fallen to the ground and the frog escaped.

But he no longer cared.

All he cared about was the girl who had just vanished in front of his eyes.

1

VICTORIA BECQUEREL

I was only here to get the cat.

And take care of a few of Grandpa Jonathan's financials.

The house was clean, but it just smelled… well… old. Musty really.

I was used to the antiseptic scent of the hospital where I worked. So much so that anything else smelled dirty.

The furry white cat jumped on top of the breakfast table as I pulled the lid on a can of cat food and set it there in front of him. I didn't care if he ate on the table.

But he just sat there and blinked at me.

"What?" I asked.

The cat meowed.

"Oh. Alright." It took me a minute to find a saucer to dump the cat food into it. I slid it over. The cat dove in, like he hadn't eaten in days.

Kit Kat. That was his name. Kit Kat sounded like a girl's name to me, but who was I to judge.

As the cat lapped up his food, I put my hands on my hips

and looked around the kitchen, trying to decide what else needed to be done.

I had vowed to never set foot here again.

But my siblings were unreachable.

My sister, Sophia, had disappeared eleven years ago, never to be found.

Just another reason for me to hate this place.

And now my other two siblings, Cameron and Mackenzie, wouldn't answer their phones. Straight to voice mail. Both of them.

What if it was important?

It was important.

Grandpa would be spending a month in rehab.

His assistant… caregiver… Tracie… had called me in tears.

Grandpa had left specific instructions that I was the one to be called in case of emergency.

Maybe because I was a doctor. Maybe because the other ones couldn't be reached and Grandpa knew it.

I'd asked Tracie to take the cat, but she said no. And no, she didn't know anyone else who could take care of him.

That's what happened when a person lived thirty minutes out of town.

You had no friends. And if you did have friends, they weren't going to spend half a day driving out to feed a cat everyday.

For an entire month.

Out of options, I'd driven here from Atlanta just to get the cat.

Just because I didn't want to be here was no reason for the cat to starve while Grandpa was in rehab.

I needed to try to see Grandpa, but what I really needed to do was to get back to Atlanta.

So I had a couple of other things to do, then I was going to throw the cat in his carrier and head out of here.

I had my reasons for not wanting to be here at the Becquerel estate. It had nothing to do with my family. Nothing to do with Grandpa.

And it had everything to do with an experience I'd had when I was just fifteen years old.

An experience I'd had in the mist.

I'd never told a single soul.

But I'd never forgotten it.

And never would.

2

GRANT LAURENT

The soil up here in the northern part of the state was good. I couldn't complain about that.

The little cotton plants were just now starting to peek up through the soil. Seeing that was my favorite part of the whole planting process. To me it was magical how the little seeds knew how to find their way out of the dirt so they could start growing into big productive plants.

Also, here in mid-March, the weather was still bearable. Pleasant even. I removed my hat to run a hand through my hair, the warm sun beating down on my head.

My horse, Fair Flax, shifted beneath me crinkling the leather of my saddle.

He shook his head at the mournful wail of a steamboat's horn as it passed. He'd heard the sound his entire life. Even down south. Maybe it was his way of greeting the boat.

I waved.

Didn't know if they could see me or not, but I waved anyway. It was the neighborly thing to do.

Somehow I'd gotten the reputation of being standoffish.

I couldn't figure out what was wrong about a man wanting to keep his head down and doing his work.

I didn't gamble or drink much or visit Natchez Under the Hill.

And I didn't dance with every marriageable girl in the county.

In fact, when I did attend a ball or picnic out of family obligation, I rarely danced at all.

Contrary to common belief, not every eligible bachelor was in need of a wife.

Now. What I could complain about was only having two acres for my cotton fields.

How exactly was a man supposed to make a success of himself with only two measly acres?

But since I did not want to be an ingrate, I kept my mouth shut about it and had been asking around to see if there was some nearby land I could purchase.

Waiting around to see what my father was going to do as far as dividing up his property between himself and his three sons was one thing. But I was not getting any younger.

The other thing I could complain about was being up here in north Mississippi to begin with.

Our plantation home outside of New Orleans had burned to the ground. Father's property to be technical. So he'd sold the land and the townhome to pay some debts.

There was supposed to be enough money left over to build a house on my mother's dowry land up here.

But Father, it seemed, at least to me, had all but decided to just live with Uncle Samuel and his wife.

Made since though, because my brother Nathan had built a home of his own for his wife and family. My other brother Andrew was doing the same. In the meantime, they lived here in the main house, but that wouldn't last for long.

My sister had a husband to take care of her and they lived in town.

That just left me.

I was accustomed to managing thousands of acres. Now I was down to two. Two acres.

Next year was going to be different.

I would figure something out.

I had not always been the serious one, I mused, as I turned Fair Flax around to head for home.

I'd actually been the mischievous one until that day long ago.

That had been the last summer I'd spent here until now.

That was the summer I'd seen the girl in the mist.

It had changed the way I saw the world.

It had changed everything about me.

And I had never told a living soul.

3

VICTORIA

I had everything ready to go.

I was ready to go.

I'd found a cat carrier in the back of Grandpa's closet and it sat out in the foyer ready for me to stick Kit Kat in there and go.

After Kit Kate finished eating, he'd disappeared, so unfortunately, I could not go until I found him.

Since he didn't go outside, it shouldn't be a problem.

"Kit Kat," I called. "Time to go."

No answer, of course.

I called him like I would call a dog. Tapped my lap and called "Here Kitty Kitty."

The cat could be anywhere. This was, after all, a three-story house.

We'd never had pets to speak of when we were growing up. Had a hound dog outside one time, but never had a cat.

I pulled out my phone. Checked the time.

If I didn't get on the road soon, I would hit rush hour traffic.

Might as well eat something now so I wouldn't have to stop later on.

Grandpa had a well-stocked refrigerator. Guess we had Tracie to thank for that.

If only she could accommodate a cat, she'd have been my new favorite person.

I pulled out a bag of ready-made salad mix and tossed it into a bowl. Sliced a tomato and a cucumber. There. Instant salad. Even easier since I didn't eat salad dressing.

I sat down at the table to eat.

Kit Kat stopped in the doorway. Licked his front paws.

"About time you showed up," I said. "Ready to go?"

While I finished my salad, the cat finished his bath.

Ready to go now, I washed my bowl and put it away.

Then I went in search of Kit Kat. I searched for thirty minutes, then gave up and went to sit on the sofa in the parlor.

The whole point of driving over here was to get the cat. I couldn't very well leave without him.

Maybe I could get him to come out by feeding him again.

I went back into the kitchen and opened another can of food.

Even emptied it out onto a saucer.

But no cat. Not this time.

Apparently Kit Kat was only interested in food on his terms.

I put my hands on my hips and waited for five minutes.

Checked the time again.

There was no way I was going to get back to Atlanta at a decent time tonight.

Sitting on the couch again, I made some calls. Asked my assistant to reschedule everything for tomorrow.

Tomorrow I would start again.

Taking my phone and my phone charger, I went upstairs to what looked like the guest room.

The house was eerie and quiet without Grandpa here.

Without anyone here.

It was too big and too creepy.

I didn't like it.

I put on my pajamas, t-shirt, and some UGGs slippers.

But before settling in, I went back downstairs to check all the doors again. This old house had far too many doors for my blood.

One door in front and one in back would have plenty for me.

Finally satisfied that everything was secure, I went back upstairs.

Kit Kat sat in the middle of the bed.

"We're leaving tomorrow," I told him. "Don't think we're not."

He just blinked at me.

I had time to figure out a new plan of attack to get this cat in his carrier.

I even thought about putting him in his carrier now. While he was sitting right here, but I couldn't do that to the little guy.

He was probably wondering where Grandpa was.

Right about now, I was wondering where Cameron and Mackenzie were.

I pulled out my phone and dialed their numbers again. One, then the other, while I absently rubbed the cat's ears. He rolled over on his back and purred.

Both went straight to voicemail.

Tomorrow, since I was still here, I'd go see Grandpa. Find out what he knew.

Surely he knew where the hell they were.

They stayed in touch with him, so he would know.

I lay in bed, staring at the ceiling, listening to the old house creak and groan.

As I wondered if it would ever go to sleep, I wondered the same thing about me.

Kit Kat, on the other hand, curled up right next to me and went to sleep.

I sighed.

Damn it.

The little cat was stealing my heart.

And my heart had only been stolen one other time.

A memory that I did a pretty good job at keeping buried deep in my brain, but being here brought back the memories.

Just more evidence that I needed to get out of here as soon as possible.

4

GRANT

The library was probably my favorite room in the house. Quiet and in shadows, it smelled like old leather and good tobacco.

As I poured myself a glass of whiskey and tossed it back, I realized I had forgotten that tonight the parents were hosting some friends from over east.

Currently in two of the guest rooms, they would be staying several days. I had actually met them once before. A middle-aged couple with three daughters. The daughters would be married now. Surely.

Taking a second glass of whiskey, this one to be savored, it settled into one of the armchairs.

The grandfather clock chimed the hour. It wouldn't be long before dinner. I was pretty sure there would be chicken on the menu tonight. I could smell it all the way from the detached kitchen.

Andrew and Mackenzie were already here and Mackenzie would be playing the piano after dinner. She was already warming up a bit. Her warming up was better than most people's actual playing.

Emma, my aunt and uncle's daughter, had been sent to finishing school for the year. Thank God.

For some unknown reason, Aunt Eloise had seen fit to have her daughter play the piano for us several nights a week. The girl had zero skill and listening to her overly happy music was torture. As my brother so aptly put it, sitting there listening to her play was like watching paint dry.

But my sister-in-law, Mackenzie played like an angel. She could have played professionally if she had wanted to. There was more to that story than I wanted to think about right now. But I could honestly say that I was looking forward to hearing Mackenzie play tonight. Her music was like balm for a troubled soul.

I would not say that my soul was troubled. I was just feeling a bit restless tonight.

Maybe it was the weather. I could feel the electricity from the storm moving in.

Strange things had been known to happen around here when there were storms.

Even when no one admitted it, I knew. I listened.

One of the advantages to keeping one's mouth closed, I had learned a long time ago, was that one learned things.

Andrew came to the door and interrupted my musings.

"Ready for dinner?" he asked. "The guests aren't coming down until later, so it's just us."

"Sure thing," I said, setting my empty glass aside. Even better. With the guests having dinner in their rooms, I would not be forced to socialize with anyone other than family.

With the echo of the grandfather clock lingering in the air, I followed my youngest brother into the dining room.

It was just seven of us. My parents. My aunt and uncle. My brother and his wife.

Normally it did not bother me to be the odd man out. To

not have anyone to share private glances with or to touch hands with beneath the table.

Sitting back with my arm over the empty table where my wife would sit—if I had one, I wondered if perhaps it might be time for me to begin looking for a wife.

When I took the basket of biscuits Mackenzie handed me, I bobbled them, spilling them all over the floor.

"I am so sorry," I said, dropping to the floor to gather up the spilled biscuits that had scattered everywhere, I took a moment to steady myself.

What had come over me?

I had never once found myself thinking that I should be looking for a wife.

5

VICTORIA

After what seemed like hours, I finally exhausted myself into a restless sleep.

But some time in the night, I woke in utter darkness.

I always kept the windows open in my high rise apartment in Atlanta, so I never woke in complete darkness. Ever.

Then I remembered that I wasn't in Atlanta. I was in the country.

And in the country, it got dark.

No street lights. Not even light from the moon.

I reached over for Kit Kat, but he'd left me.

Then, with my other hand, I reached over for my phone, but it wasn't there either. Maybe the cat knocked it off.

I wondered how long it had been since the sheets had been washed. They hadn't been so bad when I'd first climbed in to go to sleep. Maybe I just hadn't noticed. But now they smelled different. Like they had been outside.

Probably some new dryer sheet scent.

Personally, I didn't use them. Too many chemicals.

I closed my eyes, but it was too dark for me to sleep. Dark and quiet.

I jumped when a crash of thunder rumbled overhead. Ok. Maybe not so quiet.

Opening my eyes, I watched a lightning show shooting in through the window.

Thunder and lightning. And rain. Hitting the floor.

The window was open?

I got up and, unable to find my slippers, padded across the floor to the window.

Blowing rain was coming through the open window.

How the hell had the window been open?

I slammed it closed, then moved away from it. Back to the bed.

I felt around for my phone again, but couldn't find it.

I looked up just as a flash of lightning lit the room and saw myself in the mirror across the room.

I put my hands over my mouth to keep from screaming.

There was no reason to scream. There was no one here to hear me.

But I looked like a ghost. Just for an instant. I looked like a ghost and it sent my pulse racing out of control.

I needed to get out of here.

Giving up on finding my phone or my shoes, I crossed the room in my bare feet and opened the door.

And blinked against the light. Not bright overhead lights like I was used to, but dim candle light. But light nonetheless.

And there was music. Piano music.

What the—?

I stood with my hand on the doorknob and went through the possibilities.

It didn't sound like a break in. But could be kids out here using the house to party.

I shifted, trying to decide what to do.

Didn't sound like kids. Kids did not play piano music. Kids

played loud, incomprehensible music that did not sound like music to my thirty-year-old ears.

I took a deep breath and pulled the door closed behind me.

Maybe Cameron was here? Or Mackenzie?

They wouldn't know that I was here.

That was it then. Either Cameron or Mackenzie was here and, from the sounds of it, they had some friends over.

No matter which one of my siblings it was, they were going to get an earful for not answering their phone.

What was the point in having a phone if you weren't going to answer it?

Sometimes people just did not make any sense.

I slowly made my way down the hallway toward the stairs.

The storm wasn't so bad here in the hallway.

I reached the top of the stairs and looked down.

Something about the music tickled the back of my memory.

Then the music changed and I knew.

It was Mackenzie. My sister was here and she was playing her favorite melancholy song on the piano.

Well. That just figured. And here I'd been worried sick about her.

I quickly reached the bottom of the stairs and stopped. I had a clear view into the parlor.

The grandfather clock began to chime the hour.

But Mackenzie sat there at the piano. But not the Mackenzie I knew. This Mackenzie was wearing a long ballgown and had her hair pulled up on top of her head, leaving it to fall around her shoulders.

A man, dressed in some kind of tuxedo, leaned against the piano watching her every move.

A formal party. My sister was having a formal party here.

And not only was Grandpa in the rehab hospital, she had left me to deal with the whole mess by myself while she'd planned a formal party around me.

My first impulse was to march in there and give her a piece of my mind.

But that was not the way to solve problems.

Instead, I took a deep breath and counted to ten.

I would figure out how to deal with in a civilized fashion.

6

GRANT

Mackenzie was at the top of her form tonight.

Andrew had sent for a piano for her. Although I hadn't heard, it must have arrived. I'd have to ask them, because she playing even better than she had last month when I'd heard her play.

The elderly couple, Mr. and Mrs. Barnes had come down in a timely manner. I understood that they wanted to eat alone in their room tonight. They had had a long, tiring trip. I appreciated that they came down to hear Mackenzie play, especially since she had made a special trip over here tonight, precisely for their entertainment.

But from what I heard, their three daughters were still *getting ready*. Mon Dieu. By the time they finished getting ready, it would be time for Mackenzie to go home. Seemed to me like the height of rudeness and I lost some respect for Mr. and Mrs. Barnes behind it.

If I had daughters, I would make sure they had more polite social skills.

There I went again. And this time I'd added having my own

children to the mix that had started with the wayward thought about taking a wife.

That was the last thing I needed, for God's sake.

Finally, about halfway through Mackenzie's first song, one of the daughters swept into the room and took a seat in the chair next to mine.

She smiled at me, but I pretended not to see her.

The girl was thin as a beanpole and had a nose like a hawk. And even if I got past my first impression of her unattractive appearance, I most certainly did not like the way she chose to sit next to me when she could have chosen any of the empty chairs in the room.

In fact, there were three chairs lines up, specifically for the Barnes girls. No one ever sat in the chair next to mine except for Andrew. Andrew who just happened to be standing next to his wife as she played the piano.

I kept my gaze straight ahead, hoping that the girl would realize she was sitting in the wrong place and move on.

The second girl, a bit younger than the first, came in a few minutes later and sat in the middle of the three chairs that were there for them.

At least she had some basic social skills.

"My name's Ava," the girl sitting next to me said.

I grimaced, but pretended not to hear.

But apparently Ava did not take hints very well.

"She plays pretty good," Ava said.

I had to bite my tongue so much so that I swear I tasted blood.

Mackenzie was not *pretty good.* Mackenzie played like an angel. I knew of no one who could match her skill.

I wanted to tell the offensive Ava that she wouldn't know talent if it knocked her over the head, but if I did, my momma would skin me alive and I could not have that.

Ava was not worth that. Not even a little bit. I reminded

myself that the girl simply did not know any better and it wasn't her fault she was ignorant.

I'd heard Mackenzie play often enough to know that she would play three songs, then take a break, and play three more. Sometimes, if we were lucky, she would play a fourth, usually something she was learning.

That last song was usually raw and unperfect, unlike her other songs.

As Mackenzie lit into her third song, I stood up and slipped around the back, unnoticed.

I had to get away from Ava before the break if I wanted to avoid being forced into conversation with her.

She'd obviously zeroed in on me simply because I was the only male sitting alone.

I went straight into the library and stood at the window, watching the storm outside.

I'd all but forgotten about the storm between listening to Mackenzie's songs and avoiding Ava's attentions.

But here in the darkness of the library, where the curtains had been left open, it would have been impossible to miss.

I'd just stay here until Mackenzie started playing again. Then I'd go back into the parlor and find a place where I could be left alone with my own thoughts. I'd stand up if I had to.

7

VICTORIA

I stepped back, out of sight, in order to give myself time to think.

The house smelled different. Sounded different and smelled different.

It smelled like magnolias. And it sounded… alive. With the music playing and the clock ticking and just normal sounds of having people around.

A tall black man, impressively dressed all in black, approached me. Although he had an imposing demeanor, he did not look the least bit threatening.

"Good evening, Miss," he said. "My name is Villars. Might I be of assistance?"

"Yes," I said, looking up into his clear brown eyes. "That girl, playing the piano is my sister."

I had to give the man credit. Whatever part he was playing, he did it well. He barely blinked an eye.

"That's Miss Mackenzie," he said with obvious pride.

"Yes. Mackenzie. I've been… I've been looking for her."

"Yes, ma'am." He looked at me with obvious consternation. "She doesn't know you're here, does she?"

"No." I attempted to look around him, but I couldn't see inside the parlor from here. "How long has she been here?"

"Oh," Villars said. "I don't rightly know."

"I see." I had a feeling there might be something he wasn't telling me, but it didn't seem important at the time."

"If you'll come with me," he said. "I'll show you where to get something fitting to wear."

Something fitting to wear.

This must be some kind of formal dinner party.

I was beginning to think that it was a good thing I hadn't barged in only to make a fool of myself.

If nothing else, I needed to show my sister professional courtesy. She was a psychologist and these people were probably her colleagues.

If I knew my sister, she would have had this planned long before Grandpa had to suddenly go into rehab. I had no reason to be mad at her about it.

"Yes," I said. "That would be very kind of you."

"We have some things upstairs in the guest room that might suit you."

Upstairs. I had just come from there, but I followed the man right back up the stairs. He took a lantern off a table and brought it with us.

I stepped into the room after he opened it and had to press a hand against the door frame to brace myself.

I'd been mistaken. This was not the room where I had spent the night. This was more of a storage room/guest room.

There was a really big double wardrobe on one side.

Villars went straight there and opened the door on the right.

"I'll leave you to it, Miss," he said. "You can wear whatever you like."

I walked over to stand next to him and looked at the shelves and rods crammed full of different colored material.

"I don't know where to begin," I said. Looking at all this was more overwhelming than med school.

"I can send someone in to help you," he said, uncertainly, "but I'm thinking you want to keep a low profile."

"Yes," I said, with a hand on my forehead. "Don't worry. I'll figure something out."

"Yes, ma'am," he said. "just ring the bell cord if you need anything."

"Uh huh," I said, barely noticing that he left me alone with the lantern.

So many brightly colored dressed. I flipped through a few. This was not my area of expertise.

Either of my sisters would have been much more suited to this task.

My hardest decision on clothing was figuring out what color scrubs to wear.

So I reverted to what I knew. I pulled out a black dress and slipped into it. then rummaged around for a pair of boots that would fit me.

This would do, I decided as I looked at myself in the mirror. This was temporary, anyway.

I'd see what was up with my sister, find Kit Kat, and get out of here first thing in the morning.

My sister could have the house for whatever it was she needed it for.

I did not care. I just wanted to get back to Atlanta.

8

GRANT

The minute Mackenzie started playing again, I left the library and headed back to the parlor. I did what I had planned.

I stood next to the fireplace. The girl, Ava, had moved up to sit with her two sisters. Apparently, the third one had decided to come downstairs as well.

Left to my own devices, I allowed myself to get lost in the music.

I was glad my brother had married Mackenzie if for no other reason than her skill at the piano. She had a lot of other good qualities, too, but this one was definitely a bonus, at least for me.

Maybe it was because I'd spent a year listening to Emma peck away at the keys. Perhaps she'd learn to actually play while she was in finishing school. There was always hope.

I had not realized the Barnes had four daughters, but a fourth young lady had just stepped inside the parlor.

Like me, she hung back against the wall instead of taking a seat.

I quickly decided that this particular girl was not actually related to the Barnes. A friend, perhaps who had traveled with them.

She had nothing of their features. No hawk nose and was not as thin as a rail. This girl had wide eyes framed with dark lashes and plump bow shaped lips that quite simply beckoned to be kissed. Her heart-shaped face was framed by hair smooth, coffee-colored hair with choppily cut sun-kissed ends that ended just below her shoulders.

Not only had I never seen hair like that, her features were perfect.

Besides that, she held herself differently.

I took all this in about her before it registered in my besotted brain that she was dressed all in black.

Then my heart went out to her.

This young lady was in mourning. It explained her serious and aloof demeanor.

It also told me to keep my distance.

Yet, as the music ebbed and flowed around us, I could not stop looking at her.

I couldn't shake the sense that there was something vaguely familiar about her.

Something I couldn't quite grasp.

I forced myself to ignore the feeling. It was just the soft glow of candlelight in the room. The melancholy music. The rain storm outside.

Mackenzie had only played two songs, when she looked and saw the young lady in black.

Her fingers continued to move over the keys for a moment longer, then stopped.

She just stopped. Right in mid-strain.

I looked from one girl to the other.

Mackenzie obviously recognized the young lady in black.

They knew each other.

Holy crap. They could almost be sisters.

Mackenzie and Sophia had another sister. But... she was not supposed to be here.

"What's wrong?" Andrew asked as Mackenzie pushed back from the piano bench.

She merely shook her head without answering.

She reached the girl in black in about half a second and taking her hands in hers, pulled her from the room.

I wanted to follow.

But this was obvious a personal matter, so I held my ground. Waited to see what would happen next.

Unfortunately, Ava caught sight of me and headed my way.

I ducked out into the foyer again.

I didn't see the two girls, so I retreated back to the library.

It was doubtful they would go there. Uncle Samuel had a desk in there and it had somehow become a men's retreat. They would probably go to the lady's parlor. Or maybe even the kitchen.

Not my business.

9

VICTORIA

Mackenzie led me across the hall into the other parlor. This room smelled like cinnamon. A nice break from the musty smell of the rest of the house.

"What are you doing here?" She asked, turning me to face her, her unpainted nails digging into my hand.

Alarm crossed her features as her gaze swept over my gown. She was used to seeing me in scrubs, so I paid it no mind.

"Grandpa," I said.

Mackenzie put a hand over her eyes and turned away, obviously in distress.

"No," she said, turning back with tears spilling from her eyes. "When did it happen?"

I suppose she was asking when he went into rehab.

"Two days ago," I said.

"I should go," she said. "I don't know if I can, but I should go."

"Yes," I said, warming to the topic now. "You most definitely should go. You weren't there for him when he needed you. So, yes, you should go."

Mackenzie looked at me as though I had slapped her, then dropped onto a sofa.

I bit my lip. I was being too hard on her. Taking my resentment at being pulled away from my busy life to take care of Grandpa without any help.

She lowered her head and burst into tears.

Great. Now I'd done it. I could not stand tears. Not in someone I cared about. Other people, I could deal with, but not my family.

"It's okay," I said, going to sit next to her and putting my hands on her shoulders. "You couldn't have known. Don't blame yourself."

The man who had been standing next to her at the piano walked in and knelt in front of her.

He looked up at me accusingly.

"Who are you? What have you done?"

Mackenzie put a hand on his arm. "It's okay," she said. "This is my sister, Victoria." She took a breath. "Victoria, this is my husband, Andrew."

"Husband." I couldn't get out any more words. I was speechless.

When the hell had Mackenzie gotten married? No wonder I hadn't been able to get in touch with her. Was she in some kind of cult?

"Oh," Andrew said. "Well then. What have you done to Mackenzie?"

"Nothing," I said. The question was more what have you done to her.

Mackenzie looked at her husband. "She's come here with bad news."

"Bad news?" Andrew looked at her with obvious concern. Then he seemed to understand. "Your grandpa?"

"Yes," Mackenzie nodded.

I felt like I should do something to alleviate Mackenzie's obvious distress.

"It's not that bad," I said. "You can go. You can see him." I looked at Andrew. "You can both go."

"Andrew can't go," Mackenzie said, dismissively. "And I wouldn't let him anyway. It's too dangerous."

I sat down on an armchair across from them.

"I think we might be talking about two different things," I said. "I don't know what those two things are, but I do not think we're on the same page.

"You're right," Mackenzie said. "We should talk."

I nodded.

"So it happened two days ago?" She asked, her bottom lip quivering despite obviously trying to keep her composure.

I nodded.

"How?"

"I'm not sure. I didn't ask. I think he was doing something in the garden."

"He always loved that garden." Mackenzie gripped Andrew's arms and the tears started again.

I didn't say anything. Mackenzie had never been one for theatrics. She was a psychologist, for God's sake. Maybe she was drunk.

"So you came to get me?" she asked, meeting my gaze again. "That's… wow. That's very… thoughtful."

"Actually," I said. "I just came to get the cat."

10

GRANT

I had to admit that curiosity got the best of me. I poured myself another whiskey, but didn't drink it right away. Instead I took it with me when I left the library.

I was drawn to voices coming from the lady's parlor. I immediately recognized one of them as my brother Andrew's.

Since the door wasn't closed, it figured it wasn't any overly private conversation. I learned against the door frame and looked inside, trying to make sense of the situation.

Mackenzie, obviously in distress was sitting on the sofa, the woman in black sitting next to her, looking a bit helpless. Andrew knelt at Mackenzie's feet.

The older brother in me was compelled to step up. To try to help. It's what I did.

I went up to them, put a hand on my brother's shoulder and pressed the whiskey into his hands.

"Give her this," I said.

Andrew absently took the glass, but he handed it to his wife.

Mackenzie grabbed hold of it like a lifeline and downed it. I forced myself to close my mouth as Mackenzie drank the whiskey like a man.

She then took a deep breath and turned back to the girl in black. Took her hands in both of hers.

"I knew it had to happen eventually," she said. "He's in a better place. Right?"

"I guess so," the girl said, then she seemed to see me standing there.

A streak of lightning flashed across the room as our gazes met and my heart rate went through the roof.

Mon Dieu.

Even in the dim lantern light, I felt like I had just tumbled right over into her bright green eyes.

The grandfather clock ticked off the seconds as our gazes held.

Andrew had Mackenzie in his arms to console her, so neither of them noticed.

The grandfather clock began to chime the hour and I pulled myself out of my besotted haze.

"I don't believe we've met," I said, breaking the spell.

"I'm Victoria," she said.

"Victoria," I said. I had been right then. "You're Mackenzie's sister."

"Yes," she said, turning her attention back to her sister.

"How are you here?" I asked.

Mackenzie looked up at me now, with obvious pain in her eyes.

"She's come to tell me that our grandfather has died."

Victoria gasped.

"What? No." She shifted to better face her sister. "He's in the rehab hospital."

Mackenzie closed her eyes as relief swept through her.

"Why did you think that?" Victoria asked. "If you'd answer your phone, then you'd know these things."

Mackenzie looked blankly at Victoria.

"My phone…" She shook her head. "You're wearing black."

Victoria shrugged. “So?”

Mackenzie closed her eyes again. “It’s okay. Just. Just give me a minute. Okay.”

Victoria shrugged and looked back up at me.

“Do you have more of that whiskey?” she asked.

11

VICTORIA

I paced to the window, but seeing nothing more than rain pelting against the window and darkness beyond, I turned and went back to the other side of the room. Away from the lightning storm.

My plain black dress, that at first had seemed overdressed, now seemed underdressed. But I didn't think it was bad enough to cause my sister as much distress as it did.

The whole situation was more than I could comprehend.

The man, Grant, pressed a glass of whiskey in my hand, but unlike my sister, I only took a sip. It was strong. Strong drinks were not my forte, but I held onto it anyway.

Grant was looking at me as though he was trying to figure something out.

He wasn't the only one who was utterly confused.

I took another sip of the whiskey and looked at him again.

He looked like someone I should know. But I didn't know anyone here. I had not been here since I was fifteen and I didn't know any of my sister's friends.

Married. My sister had gotten married.

Maybe this some kind of role play.

"How long has my sister been married?" I asked.

"I don't know," Grant answered absently, "a few months maybe."

"I didn't know," I said.

"I would think not," he said. "since you weren't here."

Since the statement made no sense to me, I chose not to answer. It didn't sound accusatory. Just matter-of-fact.

Instead, I searched for something some other thread of conversation.

"How do you know my sister?" I asked.

"She's married to my brother," he said.

"Andrew is your brother?"

He nodded.

"I wouldn't have known." I didn't tell him, but they looked nothing alike.

Andrew looked like a kind man with an easy smile. Grant, however, looked like a brooding hero from a Victorian novel.

I studied him over the rim of my whiskey glass.

He was a handsome man with chiseled features. Strong was the one word that came to mind. A strong, handsome man.

"Would you like to sit down?" he asked.

And a gentleman. I could tell he was a gentleman. Thoughtful. Probably the older brother, too.

"I would, but I think my sister is looking for me," I said.

"Good luck," he said as I walked off.

"Thanks," I said, turning around as I walked off.

I had a flash back to that day fifteen years ago.

That day when I'd taken a walk and had come face to face with a boy.

Nonsense. Being here. In this house. It was natural that I would have flashbacks to that event that had left me shaken to the core.

I shook it off and went to sit next to my sister.

Andrew joined Grant across the room and spoke in hushed tones.

"Sit," Mackenzie said. "I think there's something you need to know."

I sat and Mackenzie took my hands.

"How are you?" she asked.

"I'm okay. I'm supposed to be at work, but..." I scowled at her. "Where have you been? You and Cameron both. Why don't you answer your phones?"

"We can't," she said.

How was she being so calm?

"Have you joined a cult?" I asked, leaning forward so only she could hear me.

That's what it had to be.

"No," she laughed. "It's nothing that easy."

I didn't see how a cult was easy, but I needed to give her time to settle from the shock of thinking Grandpa had passed away and tell me what was going here.

I looked over my shoulder at Grant.

And he was looking at me.

12

GRANT

"They said she would never come here," Andrew said. "to the past."

I pulled my gaze away from Victoria's back to my brother's. Victoria was trouble. I knew it in my bones.

"I think it was an accident," I said.

"How could that happen when she never comes here to this house?"

"Think about it," I said, taking my brother's arm. "Let's step out onto the veranda."

The rain was slow and steady now that the storm had passed. The breeze was nice and cool. A nice change from being inside.

"Three of her siblings have vanished," I said. "The grandfather knows about the time travel, but did they tell Victoria?"

"I don't think so," Andrew said, watching his wife through the window.

"I don't either," I said, taking a cigar out of my pocket.

"Is that one of mine?" Andrew asked.

"No." I looked down at the cigar.

"Here," Andrew reached into his pocket and took out two cigars. "Try this."

I sniffed the cigar. "Not bad," I said, mostly to annoy my brother.

But he wasn't really listening to me. He was busy watching Mackenzie.

"She doesn't know she's in the past."

That got Andrew's attention.

"Good God," Andrew said, looking at me now. "What are we going to do about that?"

"We?" I looked through the window at the sisters. "Not we. Her sister will take of it."

"Then there's Cameron and Sophia," he said.

"She's going to be in for quite a shock." I said, with a nod, trying to resist my natural instinct to take responsibility for her. "She has a niece, too."

"And two on the way."

"Two? What the—?" I looked questioningly at Andrew. "Sophia… and…"

"Yes." He smiled sheepishly.

I grinned and clapped my brother on the back.

"Congratulations," I said, holding up my cigar. "We should light these things in celebration."

"Absolutely," he said.

Ava stepped outside the front door, saw me, and smiled.

I groaned, turning my back to her. "I need to disappear."

Andrew laughed.

"I'm glad you find humor in my misery."

"I know how to fix it," Andrew said.

"How?" I asked. "Anything that doesn't involve Fair Flax?"

"Absolutely," he said with a glance toward the sisters sitting inside on the sofa.

"Her?" I asked with my gaze on Victoria. "No way." But even as I said the words, I knew that deep in my heart I rather liked the idea.

And besides, desperate times called for desperate measures.

13

VICTORIA

I barely even tasted the whiskey, but it burned all the way down… and up… making my eyes burn.

Mackenzie set her empty glass aside and leaned toward me.

"Alright," she said. "I have a LOT to tell you."

"Seems like it," I said.

Seeming to consider where to start, she tapped her fingers on the skirt of her light blue dress. She seemed to be wearing it so naturally. As though she wore dresses like this all the time.

"I think I'll just jump in and cut to the chase," she said. "Then we'll work backwards."

I braced myself.

"I think you're gonna want another one of those." She nodded toward my empty glass.

"I'm good," I said, but before I could get the words out good, Victoria was motioning toward her husband.

Her husband.

Good God.

Had I really been that deep into work?

I stayed in touch with my siblings… didn't I?

Obviously not so much.

Andrew and Grant stood in front of us. Grant watched me.

Mackenzie held up her glass and, taking mine, held it up, too.

"We're going to need more of this," she said.

"We'll be right back," Andrew said, starting to turn.

When Grant didn't move, Andrew grabbed him by the arm and pulled him along, too.

Mackenzie leaned forward again.

"This is 1854," she said.

I looked blankly at her. Then looked around the room.

It could be. The way the house looked. The ticking of the grandfather clock drifting through the house. The way everyone was dressed.

But… no.

I shook my head.

"I know you don't believe me," she said, but let me back up and start from the beginning.

Andrew and Grant were back with drinks.

Andrew handed Mackenzie hers and Grant handed me my glass. Our fingers brushed ever so slightly, but that light touch sent tremors all through me.

And I had a clear image of that day I'd seen the boy standing in the mist.

I jerked my hand back, nearly spilling the whiskey, but Grant kept it steady.

As I gazed into his blue eyes, I could barely catch my breath.

A skinny girl with a hawkish nose walked by.

"Do you mind if I sit with you?" Grant asked.

"Looks like you could use protecting," I said, with a little smile.

"You have no idea."

He slid a chair over and sat down next to me. Andrew did the same to sit next to Mackenzie.

After the skinny girl left the room, Andrew got up and closed the door, leaving the four of us alone.

"Cameron should be here to tell you this," Mackenzie said. "He's much better at telling a story than I am."

Sitting here like this reminded me of my childhood. When Cameron used to tell us creepy bedtime stories when we were all supposed to be sleeping.

"It started in the 1700s," Mackenzie said, pulling my attention back to her. "1714 to be exact."

14

GRANT

I sat next to Victoria. Close enough that when she sat back, I could smell the faint scent of magnolia in her hair.

I knew most of the story about Vaughn Dupree and the time travel, but every time someone recounted it, I heard something different. Something I hadn't heard before. Or something put another way that filled in a gap.

No matter what she said, Mackenzie's voice was mesmerizing as she told her sister the story.

It was shocking to me that two of Victoria's sisters and her brother and her grandmother had all traveled through time, yet she knew nothing about it.

"Because our grandmother Vaughn's parents were killed when Vaughn was very young, she was raised by nuns in a convent. But she could not stay there forever.

"Americans began requesting wholesome girls who would make good wives. They were called casket girls. We would call them mail order brides.

"So Vaughn traveled to America to marry a man she had

never met. She was almost to her destination—Natchez—when her traveling party was attacked.

"Everyone, even her best friend Mary, was killed by hostile Indians."

As Mackenzie took a moment to take a sip of whiskey, a rumble of thunder echoed over us. We sat in silence. Waiting for Mackenzie to continue.

"Fortunately, there was a kind old Indian who saved her life. He cast a spell that made a rip in time. She went through that rip in time and landed in the 1800s.

"There was one major problem though. And the old Indian even warned her about it."

She paused for effect. None of us moved a muscle.

"The rip in time never healed. Not only did Vaughn continue to travel back and forth through time during her lifetime, but so did… do… those of her blood."

"What does that mean?" Victoria asked.

Mackenzie blinked at her sister. "It means that we..." She motioned between them. "Also travel through time because we're her descendants."

"So all the Becquerels?" Victoria asked.

Mackenzie nodded and took a small sip of whiskey.

"What about Grandpa? He's a Becquerel."

"He's not one of Vaughn's descendants," Mackenzie said, looking at her sister blankly.

"Don't try to think about it too hard," Andrew said. "It'll give you a headache."

Mackenzie shot him a scathing glance.

"What?" he asked. "It's true. You told me that yourself on more than one occasion."

Victoria looked at me. I got the sense she was searching for something. Maybe looking for my reaction to all this.

I wanted to reach out to her. To take her hand. But after the tremors that had shot through me after our hands just barely touched a few minutes ago, I was reluctant to do so.

"Do you believe her?" Victoria asked me.

This was the first time anyone had asked me that and the question caught me off-guard.

It actually took me a second to know how to answer her.

I'd seen so much. Heard so much.

"Yes," I said. "I do believe her."

I believed every word of it, especially looking into Victoria's eyes.

She was like no one I had ever met. It was easy for me to know that she was not of this time. No one in this time had skin as smooth as her. Hair as beautiful.

Her sisters did. But no one else.

I did believe in time travel.

15

VICTORIA

As I listened to Mackenzie's story—a story she and the two men sitting with us obviously believed was the truth, I found myself distracted by Grant.

The dark brooding man carried a large presence and he smelled like a mixture of whiskey, horses, and something I couldn't readily identify.

I could not shake the feeling that he was somehow familiar to me. That I should know him. Or that, at the least, I had seen him before. Maybe I had even heard his voice.

But I was being fanciful.

This house. The storm. Finding my sister here in a time that she adamantly claimed was 1854. My sister was the most logical person I knew. Even more logical than I was. She worked with crazy people all day long.

I couldn't help but wonder how she had come around to accepting such a far-fetched notion as time travel.

Mackenzie told me that Cameron was here, too. That he was married and lived in town with his wife. Sophia lived here, too, in her own house with her husband and child.

The knowledge that I was an aunt was almost more

disconcerting than the whole notion that we had all traveled through time.

"Does Grandpa know about this?" I asked, interrupting whatever Mackenzie was saying.

"Yes," she said. "He helped us. All of us."

"Why didn't someone tell me about it?"

"We were going to," she said. "Cameron especially was going to. Do you remember when he asked all of us to come out to Grandpa's house? But we were too busy to make it."

"Vaguely," I said, though I really didn't. I stayed busy morning and night.

I hadn't even tried to hide my annoyance when Tracie had called to tell me that Grandpa was in the rehab hospital.

The storm had passed and the rain had turned to little more than a mist.

I must have been thinking about all this too much because my head hurt.

Well, Andrew had warned me, hadn't he?

"I need to take a walk," I said, standing up.

Both Grant and Andrew stood up also. I looked at Mackenzie, but she just shrugged.

"Welcome to the nineteenth century," she said.

"I'll go with you," Grant said as I stepped past them.

"There's no need," I said with a little smile. "I'm sure I'll be perfectly safe."

Mackenzie and Andrew exchanged a glance.

"What?" I asked. "I've done everything by myself. Travel—"

"Victoria," Mackenzie interrupted. "This is 1854. There are dangers you have never had to be aware of."

"Like what?" I asked, crossing my arms.

"Well… Indians."

I felt the blood drain from my face.

"Indians?" Surely this was some kind of joke. But no one looked the least bit amused.

"Fine," I said, sweeping past them in what I hoped was an elegant manner. But it was doubtful considering I had never worn a dress like this, much less swept past anyone.

Drake was beside me in an instant.

As we stepped outside the door, he held out an arm.

"It's customary for a lady to take a gentleman's arm," he said in response to my blank glance.

Knowing it was not a good idea, I put my arm in the crook of his elbow.

There was no tremor like there had been when I'd touched his bare hand, but it was trouble.

And I knew it just as sure as I knew how to set a broken arm.

16

GRANT

Victoria wasn't the only one who could use some fresh air.

The ground was moist after the rain and the moon shone bright and big over the tops of the oak trees.

"Would you like to sit?" I asked, with a nod toward the porch swing.

"Is it customary?" she asked with a smile playing about her lips.

"Very much," I grinned. I liked this girl.

After she removed her hand from my arm, I held the swing while she sat down. Then I sat down next to her.

"This world must be fraught with dangers," she said. "for a girl to need so much hovering."

"I don't think it's that, so much," I said. "as it is being a gentleman."

"How so?"

I scratched my cheek, considering.

"Which would you rather?" I asked. "Have me here paying attention to you, even if it is by using the excuse of holding the swing for you. Or would you rather me go stand over there and look out at the moon?"

"I see your point," she said. "If you're just going to stand there, you may as well go back inside."

"Exactly," I said. "And what would you think of me." I'm not sure if I intended that to be a question or a statement, but it came out as a statement.

She didn't answer, but she did smile to herself as she wrapped her fingers around the rope that held the swing in the air.

"What's customarily next?" she asked.

"Good question." I leaned back in the swing. "I don't court."

"What?" she asked, turning to face me. "You mean you don't date?"

I shook my head, assuming I knew what she was asking me.

She turned away to look at the moon, but I could see that she was thinking.

"Are we courting?" she asked. I heard a faint trace of amusement in her voice. Since I didn't know what that meant, I chose to ignore it.

"Maybe," I said.

She nodded.

An owl flew onto a nearby oak tree limb and asked our identity while frogs called for more rain. The storm had passed and things were back to normal.

"But you have brothers and a sister. So you know what's involved in courtship."

"I don't have to have brothers and sisters to know that one."

"Good to know." She was definitely smiling now. "So tell me, Grant. Why don't you court? As the oldest, shouldn't you be married?"

"How did you know I was the oldest?" I asked, looking at her sideways.

“A girl needs to know things about a man before she goes out into the night with him.”

“Good point,” I said.

“But you didn’t answer my question. Why don’t you court?”

“I had things to do first. I want to be successful in my own right. Not just ride on my father’s coattails.”

“What does that have to with courting?” she persisted. “Are you—do you prefer the company of men?”

“I’m beginning to worry about the future of this country.” I glanced over at her. “But no. I do not prefer the company of men. I figure when I find the woman for me, I’ll just marry her. No need courting a woman I already know doesn’t suit me.”

She was smiling again.

And I would have loved to know what she was thinking right about now.

17

VICTORIA

I had not intended to enjoy this evening so much. Not at all, really.

I'd come here to this house. Simply to pick up Grandpa's cat.

But. Oh my. I had found so much more.

I had found my sister and if what she told me was true, I now knew why she did not answer her phone.

Apparently, my brother was also here. Somewhere in this time.

Mackenzie almost talked about this time like it was a place. A place without cell phone service. Like driving up into the mountains.

Her response to something happening to Grandpa was to go to him.

There were many things unanswered.

Was she saying she had a choice? That she had chosen to be here in the past?

She'd also said that Grandpa had helped them get here.

So my logical conclusion was that, yes, she and Cameron and even Sophia were in the past because they chose to be here.

Perhaps Mackenzie could tell me how to get home. Back to my own time.

They may have chosen to live in the past… and in the country… but I couldn't see that ever being my choice.

I was a city girl. A high rise condo in Atlanta. Computers. Cell phones. Everything technological and modern.

But I could take an evening. An evening to enjoy the company of a man that I found entertaining.

Part of what I found entertaining was, of course, the novelty of him being a man of 1854. Supposedly.

I had not boarded this train with both feet. I reserved the option to decide that this was, actually, a cult of some kind.

"So my assessment of you being the strong silent type was accurate," I said.

"Is there something wrong with those qualities in your time?"

"No." I shook my head. "Not at all. But it's not so common in the future as it is now."

"I wonder why," he said.

"I could tell you," I said. "but I don't think you would get it."

"I'm smarter than I look," he said, sitting up and straightening his jacket.

I laughed.

"Okay," I said. "Well for one thing, we're taught that it's best to be balanced."

He looked at me sideways.

"Men are taught to open up and show their feminine side while women are taught to be more masculine." I explained.

He was frowning now.

"What are you trying to say?"

"It's supposed to be healthy for men to show their feelings. That's their feminine side. And on the flip side, it's good for men and women to be strong and independent."

"You're wrong," he said.

I nodded. I'd expected as much. Our cultures were too different.

"I do get it," he said.

"You get it?" I wasn't quite sure I believed him.

"Who do you think runs these massive households? The women. And who writes all the sad songs? The men."

Well hell. Maybe our cultures weren't as different as I'd assumed.

18

GRANT

I honestly hadn't expected to have anything to talk about with a woman from the future. It had baffled me how my siblings had fallen in love with a person from another century.

Just like that. What could they possibly have found to talk about? What common ground had they found? Had it all been physical?

And yet Victoria and I had found so much to talk about. We hadn't had a single moment of awkward silence.

She was hands down the most intelligent woman I had ever had a conversation with. I couldn't see how we would ever run out of things to talk about.

Unfortunately, Victoria's sister had other ideas.

"Hey," she said, coming to the door. "We're about to head upstairs. Get some rest. But first I need to find you a room."

"I'm good," Victoria said. "I have a room. The guest room."

Mackenzie stood her ground. Glanced at me.

"You should know that it's customary for men and women to have chaperones when spending time together."

"Oh," Victoria said. "I see."

She looked at me, but I just shrugged. I couldn't deny it.

"I guess I'll say goodnight then," she said.

Before she stood up, she leaned over and lowered her voice.

"How is it customary for us to say goodnight?" she asked.

I stood up and held out my hand to help her up from the swing.

Smiling, she put a hand in mine and stood up.

With our hands linked, everything else faded away and I flashbacked to that day in the road beneath the oak trees. That day in the mist. The day I decided I would never come back here.

She was no longer smiling either. Instead she was looking at me as though she had seen a ghost.

Now that she was standing, I released her hand. I had to.

I was far too overcome with those emotions she thought I wouldn't feel simply because I was a man.

Since she appeared to be frozen to the floor, I offered my elbow for her to put her hand and led her to the door where I handed her off to her sister.

Then I bowed low. "Good night," I said.

"Good night," she repeated softly, her eyes moist.

"There's more to the custom, but I think it can wait until tomorrow," I said.

"Good idea." Then she turned around and followed her sister inside, across the parlor to the foyer.

I stood where I was.

When things kept repeating themselves, they could no longer be considered coincidence.

Two times I'd touched her hand and two times I'd flashed back to that day in the mist.

It was as though we had made a silent promise to each other.

A promise that had been made fifteen years ago.

19

VICTORIA

"Are you sure you're alright?" Mackenzie asked as we went up the stairs.

The grandfather clock's chimes echoed through the whole house.

I shivered. No. I'm not alright.

"Yes," I said. "of course." I looked over at her. "Considering that I've gone back in time several hundred years."

Mackenzie took my explanation at face value as she left me at the door to my bedroom.

"Are you sure you don't need anything?" she asked.

"I'm sure," I lied. "Thank you." Then I hugged her. I wasn't sure how long it had been since I'd seen my sister, but it had been too long.

Then I turned away quickly and went into my room, closing the door behind me.

Truth was. I needed a lot of things.

Electricity would be a good start.

A bathroom with running water.

I went over and looked out the window at the full moon

hovering over the oak trees. Oak trees that were not nearly as big as they had been.

I backed away from the window.

That realization nearly took me to my knees.

I dropped into the armchair that fortunately wasn't far away.

Here, right in front of me, was irrefutable proof that I had indeed gone back in time.

No one could reduce the size of trees. Not even a cult.

With a glance around the room, I saw other things that weren't as they should be. The room was bigger because there was no bathroom. No closet. Just a wardrobe on one wall.

It could all be an illusion, I thought, desperate to grasp onto a logical explanation. Smaller trees. Larger bedroom. Something in my drink, perhaps.

But I had no more symptoms of being drugged.

Just some illusions.

Maybe seeing my sister was an illusion, too.

No. That did not seem likely.

I tucked the idea of illusions away to think about another time.

There was something else even more concerning.

Each time I touched Grant's hand, I had a flashback to that day in the mist.

The day I had vowed to never return here. Something was far too inexplicable. I preferred cold hard science.

That was the day I'd seen a boy in the mist. Touched his hand.

Everything around us had vanished. No wind. No sounds. It had been like floating in a vortex.

Then he had vanished.

And everything had gone back to normal.

Except it hadn't.

I had regular dreams. Not nightmares. Just disconcerting

dreams. I could still see the boy clearly… the mist swirling around us.

He had been but a boy.

Yet… I could see the boy's features in Grant. But was it merely my imagination? It had been so long ago that it was hard to know.

Fifteen years was a long time ago.

I sighed. Perhaps things would look different in the light of day.

20

GRANT

I got up early the next morning, saddled Fair Flax, and rode out to my two acres.

Today would be a good day to go into town. Meet with the attorney I had hired to assist me in making inquiries about expanding my property. A man could not make a success with just two acres of cotton.

My next oldest brother had started his own business venture a couple of years ago. He was that much further ahead. He'd not only built his own house where he lived with his wife and child, but was also in the process of building a textile mill on the riverbank. A mill where he could weave raw cotton into cloth. It was brilliant, really. What was the point of sending our cotton north, having it turned into cloth, then shipped back to us?

That whole process handicapped the south. We grew our own cotton. It made no sense to have to pay to have cloth made from that very same cotton shipped back to us.

My youngest brother Andrew was content experimenting with his tobacco plants. He had plans to expand also, but he did not seem so concerned about rushing into building his own house.

Perhaps it was because I was the oldest. Living in my uncle's home... with my parents... was not enough for me.

Things had been going well when we'd lived down south. I'd had hundreds of acres to manage. Then the house had burned and everything had turned upside down.

I could have stayed in New Orleans, sure.

But I put family above all else. And my family had needed me.

Without family, we had nothing.

The ground was soft from last night storm and Fair Flax kicked up little clumps of mud as I rode toward my plot of land.

I rode straight up to a little knoll where I could look over my two acres. My father had done us right when he'd given us land that bordered the Mississippi River. It was a piece of starter property.

It wasn't that I didn't appreciate it.

It was just that I harbored quiet ambitions. Some men boasted about what they were going to do. Not me. I kept my mouth shut and my head down.

I was a doer. Not a talker.

The thought brought a smile to my face.

Victoria had called me the strong silent type. She'd hit that nail right on the head.

That was a most accurate description for me. And it was interesting that it had come from someone I had just met.

I nudged Fair Flax down the hill to walk among the plants. They had practically doubled in size with last night's rain.

A miracle of nature.

This was good land. I could make a home here.

I could build a house here that overlooked the river. It was too high up to flood.

Sophia, my brother's wife from the future, could design it for me. Even with a baby to take care of, she still dabbled in architectural designs. It was something she had done in the future. Something she was good at.

Meeting Victoria had changed my perspective. Almost like it had shaken something loose in my head. Something I had been shoving down for years now.

And it all started with an unspoken promise in the mist.

21

VICTORIA

I woke with sunlight across my face. It took about a tenth of a second for the events of last night to coming rushing back.

I was used to odd sleeping hours and even grabbing a quick nap on a bed somewhere in the back of a hospital where waking up and quickly getting oriented was second nature.

But this was not a hospital. Instead of an antiseptic scent, it smelled like magnolias.

A rooster crowed outside my open window. Certainly not a sound I ever heard waking up in my Atlanta high rise.

Then I heard a sound that sent a chill down my spine. The mourning horn of a steamboat. Long and deep, echoing off the water. The sound reminded me of that day.

My sisters were taking a nap and my brother was somewhere else. I couldn't remember where.

But since I hadn't been sleepy, I'd wanted to go outside and see things. I had just been able to catch a glimpse of the Mississippi River from the upstairs balcony, but I'd wanted to see it up close. Wanted to see the steamboats packed with tourists as they floated past.

Such was the logic of an adventurous fifteen-year-old girl.

I took a deep breath and slowly let it out. I was here. I'd had no choice but to come back to Grandpa's house.

Hadn't I closed that window?

I was not in Grandpa's house. At least as I knew it.

I was still in the alternate reality that my sister insisted was 1854.

The air felt different. Definitely not climate controlled. And one glance outside at the trees, confirmed it.

I was in the past.

My next thought was of Grant.

Good heavens. I was crushing on a man from the nineteenth century.

This could not be healthy.

And the worst part. Mackenzie was a psychologist.

My sister—the psychologist—had put me in this situation. I needed to have a talk with her.

But first I needed to get up and get dressed. I'd slept in my own pajama bottoms and t-shirt, but I needed something to wear for the day.

I wasn't sure if I was supposed to go into the storage closet to find something to wear or not. I rather liked my black dress, even though it was indicative of mourning in this time.

I could see the progression of how that had changed. Black went from the color representing mourning to the color representing formality. Since mourning was formal.

Made sense.

I pulled off my pajamas and put on the hoop skirt, then pulled the dress over my head. After getting dressed, I sat down at the vanity and brushed my hair.

I took my time, reflecting on what I was supposed to do.

I had no answer. There was no definitive plan. No right answer.

All I could do was talk to my sister. See if she had some method that would send me back to the future.

Perhaps I could see my brother, Cameron, before I left. And my sister Sophia.

Geez.

Now I was thinking about this time as a place to visit.

It was not a place to visit.

It was another dimension.

A forgotten time.

22

GRANT

Back at the barn, I unsaddled Fair Flax and brushed him down, taking my time.

Andrew came in to saddle up his own horse. He was heading out as I headed in.

He tossed a blanket over his horse.

"What did you think about Victoria?" he asked.

"I don't know what to think." I picked up one his hooves and brushed out the dirt. "Mackenzie must have been really surprised to see her."

"Yeah," Andrew said. "She's worried about her grandfather. They got really close before she came here."

I let the horse put his foot down. Leaned over him to look at Andrew.

"Do you ever find it strange?" I asked. "That three siblings traveled to the past to marry three people who are also siblings?"

"Sometimes," Andrew said, putting a saddle over his horse, named Lightning Bug. Our sister had named the horse years ago and it stuck. "But mostly I'm just grateful that I found Mackenzie. She's everything to me."

"I know." I went back to brushing Fair Flax.

The leather saddle creaked as Andrew tightened the straps.

"That just leaves you," he said.

I looked up, not bothering to hide the scowl on my face.

"What's that supposed to mean?" I asked.

Andrew, never daunted by my moods, just grinned.

"Well, think about it. Three out of four siblings travel from the future to the past where they marry three of out four siblings. That just leaves Victoria. And you. A match made in heaven."

"You're talking nonsense," I said. "It doesn't work that way."

But hadn't I just been thinking the exact same thing?

"Some things are just destined," Andrew shrugged.

Thinking it and hearing it out loud were entirely two different things.

And I wasn't ready to hear it out loud. I was still becoming accustomed to thinking about it in my head.

Just because Victoria was the most beautiful and interesting woman I had ever met, didn't mean I was to announce to the world that I wanted to marry her.

Andrew grabbed his reins and started out, Lightning Bug in tow.

"Victoria and Mackenzie are in the parlor," he said over his shoulder. "I think they're sending for Cameron and Sophia. For dinner tonight. It'll be the whole family."

I grumbled something at my brother's back.

This had nothing to do with me.

I'd just stay away from the parlor until I got my head straightened out.

There was a way for Victoria to return to the future. And between the four of them, they would figure it out. They were all bright, intelligent people.

As soon as Victoria finished with her family reunion, she'd be ready to go back to her own time.

I'd heard someone say that she was a doctor in her time. She would definitely be ready to get back to her own life.

And she would want nothing to do with a simple farmer who lived in the past.

23

VICTORIA

I sat in the kitchen at the breakfast table with Mackenzie. The other women were in the parlor doing needlepoint. I think they were just giving Mackenzie and me some privacy. A kind gesture.

Mrs. Laurent, Grant's mother, had brought us a plate of scones and left it on the table.

I couldn't stop glancing toward the door, hoping to catch a glimpse of Grant.

If Mackenzie noticed… which I'm sure she did... Nothing got past her. She didn't say anything.

I forced myself to focus on what she was saying.

"There is a way," she said. "but you can't do it."

"Why not?" I asked. No. No. She said there was a way back. There had to be a way back.

"Because you don't have the key."

"I have to get back," I said, fear running up and down my spine. "Kit Kat is there by himself. No food. No water. No one to take care of him."

Mackenzie was looking at me with her most concerned expression. Like I was a distressed client. Maybe I was.

"Surely someone will go by," she said. "feed him."

I shook my head, taking a deep breath. I looked outside at the oak trees that weren't as tall as they should be.

"So if I had the key, what would I do?"

Mackenzie just looked at me.

"It can't hurt to tell me," I said. After all, knowledge was power. And who knows when I might need to know.

Mackenzie leaned forward. Her hair falling forward across her cheeks.

She looked really, really good. This time suited her. The dress and the hair made her look so much more feminine.

"Okay. I'm going to quote it exactly," she said. "Put the key in the clock. Then in the second between the lightning flash and following thunder, turn the clock back one hour."

I looked blankly at her.

Mackenzie shook her head. "I told you it wouldn't mean anything."

"No," I said. "It could. All I need is the key."

"The key is in the clock. In the future." She picked up a scone and bit off the end of it.

"How do you know this?"

"Because…" she said, looking me point blank in the eyes. "I left it there."

"Why?"

"Because when it came right down to it, I didn't need it. Love brought us together."

The back door opened and I heard footsteps coming this way. Heavy, male footsteps.

I looked right at the door.

Grant stepped through the doorway, his gaze down as he pulled off his leather work gloves, not seeing me at first.

I knew the moment he looked up and saw me.

He stopped, his feet frozen to the floor. Our gazes locked and my breath came in shallow gasps.

My heart rate was high, much too high.

"Good morning," he said.

"Good morning," I said.

Mackenzie sat quietly, not saying anything.

"Did you sleep well?" he asked.

"I did actually," I said, instinctively pressing a finger against my wrist to check my pulse.

Counting my heart beats gave me something to focus on and was actually calming.

Grant went to the stove and filled a cup with what passed for coffee.

My own cup sat on the table in front of me, barely touched. One little sip and I was done with it. Unless it was a skinny macchiato with extra caramel, I had no use for it. Not going to drink what I imagined motor oil tasted like.

Maybe later, when I needed a caffeine hit, I'd give it another go. Surely there was some cane sugar around here somewhere to sweeten the taste.

Mackenzie was drinking some kind of tea.

"Do you find it a lot different from sleeping in the future?" he asked, leaning against the counter.

It was as though we were alone, just the two of us having a conversation.

"I didn't notice," I said. "Until I woke up this morning. There are no roosters where I lived."

Mackenzie laughed. "That's an understatement."

Grant and I both looked at her. She cleared her throat.

"She lives… in the city… and not on the first floor."

I was impressed with Mackenzie's diplomacy. She had obviously done well adapting what she knew about to future into language that people in the past could understand.

I started to elaborate, but smiled instead. There would be plenty of time to elaborate… if I stayed here after tonight.

Grant bobbled his cup as I smiled at him, but quickly recovered.

I liked the way he was looking at me.

As though I was the only woman he'd ever been attracted to.

And ever would be.

I worked around male doctors all day long and I knew the different ways a man could look at a woman.

The way he was looking at me was something I didn't see very often.

Trouble.

Grant was trouble.

24

GRANT

So much for my plan to stay away from Victoria.

Now that I had seen her again, I didn't want to leave her.

When she'd smiled, I'd nearly come undone. It would have been most humiliating to spill coffee all over myself just because a girl smiled at me.

Her smile that held so many secrets. Secrets I wanted to discover.

But I knew enough about women to know that discovering her secrets would take time. A lot of time. Especially since she was from the future.

She was like Sophia and Mackenzie. I never expected to understand them. But they were my brother's wives, so I didn't have to. Shouldn't, in fact. It wouldn't be fitting.

Neither of the girls thought to invite me to sit with them. Something I'd discovered about women from the future. They were informal and didn't think about such things as invitations to have a seat.

So I pulled out a chair and sat down—without an invitation.

"I heard you're having your whole family over tonight," I said, taking a sip of what passed as coffee.

That was one thing about New Orleans. The coffee was better. And the food was better. Up here in the north, people didn't seem to know how to make food taste good. It was baffling really.

"That's the plan," Victoria said, tapping a finger on one of the letters sitting on the table.

"Someone has to deliver the message to my brother in town."

"Is there no one available?" I asked.

"A messenger boy," Mackenzie said. "Took one over to Sophia. When he gets back, he can run this one into town for Cameron."

I pulled out my pocket watch and checked the time.

"It'll be late," I said. "The sooner he and Isabella get the message, the more likely they are to make it."

Victoria just looked at me, but Mackenzie nodded. "I know."

"Nathan would have taken it," Victoria said. "but he had a meeting of some sort."

"I can take it," I said, draining my coffee.

"I couldn't ask you to do that," Victoria said.

"I don't mind," I said. "I have to pick up a couple of things in town anyway."

"That's very kind of you." Mackenzie, ignoring her sister's glance, slid the letter in my direction.

I took the letter and put it in my pocket.

Then I turned my attention back to Victoria.

"Do you ride?" I asked.

"Ride?"

"Horseback."

"No." She shook her head.

"Then we can take the buggy," I said. "If you want to go with me."

I think she was going to say yes, but then seemed to think better of it.

"Isn't that against one of the rules?" she asked, looking at her sister. "Being alone with a man?"

"I think it'll be okay," Mackenzie said. "It's daylight."

"I don't understand these rules," she murmured, mostly to herself.

"They're there to protect your reputation," Mackenzie told her.

I looked at Mackenzie with a raised eyebrow. Surely she did not think I would put her sister's reputation at risk.

I wouldn't want to be forced into a duel with anyone.

She would be perfectly safe.

And Mackenzie knew it.

25

VICTORIA

Although I didn't say it out loud, I did not plan to be here long enough to establish a reputation, good or bad.

I pushed the motor oil coffee aside and looked at Grant.

"Yes," I said. "I'll go with you." That way I could see Cameron sooner. Without having to wait until tonight.

"You can't wear that," Mackenzie said, with a glance at my black dress.

"Why not? I like this dress."

"She'll be okay," Grant said. "In fact, the black dress will keep people from gossiping so much about us being together."

"I should just go with you both," Mackenzie said.

"No."

"Not necessary."

Grant and I answered at the same time.

"Fine," Mackenzie sat back, holding up her hands. "I can see when I'm not wanted." She pretended to be offended, but I saw the smile playing about her lips.

Surely she understood that I wanted to spend some extra time with Cameron.

"But that is not a riding dress and I can't in good conscience allow you to wear it into town."

"Whatever," I said. "Fine."

"I'll go get the horse and buggy ready," Grant said. "Then I'll come back here for you."

"Sounds good," I said, moving to stand up. Grant stood up, too. "Guess we're headed to the clothing closet then."

"It won't take long to change," Mackenzie said, standing up, too.

I watched Grant as he walked purposely from the room.

"He's a good man," Mackenzie said.

"I can see that," I said.

"Don't mess with his emotions," she said.

"I don't know what you're talking about."

We left the kitchen and started toward the stairs.

The grandfather clock was already tolling the hour. Though it was still creepy, I was getting used to it.

"I know you aren't planning on staying here," Mackenzie said. "Don't let him get too attached to you."

"And how, exactly, do I prevent that from happening?"

Mackenzie just rolled her eyes.

"I know you're a serial dater," she said.

"I am not." I said, aghast that she would say such a thing.

Mackenzie stopped at the foot of the stairs and glared at me with her hands on her hips.

"When is the last time you had a boyfriend who lasted more than one season?"

I had to stop and think. First of all, what did she mean by one season?

"My point exactly," Mackenzie said.

"You really like this family," I said, hoping I did a decent job of hiding my jealousy that Mackenzie had found her family.

Besides, I liked them, too.

"Of course, I do," she said, pulling up her long skirt enough that she didn't trip over it. "I'm married to Grant's brother and we're going to have a baby."

"Wait," I said. "you're pregnant?"

She nodded.

"When were you going to tell me this?"

"I wanted to make sure."

I reached out. Put a hand over hers.

"I saw you drinking whiskey."

"Not whiskey. Tea. It looks like whiskey though."

"Why?"

"Keeps people from asking too many questions. They would notice and I didn't want to answer."

We walked in silence the rest of the way up the stairs.

It seemed like a lot of time was spent worrying about how others would perceive people of this time and what they did.

I didn't say anything though. It was important for my sister to be happy. And I could tell she was doing what she needed to do in order to adapt to this world. This way of life.

I just knew that I wouldn't be able to do it.

As we reached the landing window, Mackenzie had moved ahead. I slowed to look out the window.

Just as I was turning the corner, Grant passed by below. Slowing, he gazed up at me. He tipped his hat and grinned.

My heartrate shot into overdrive again.

My sister was worried about me messing with Grant's emotions.

I was beginning to think that it might be just the opposite.

26

GRANT

I had the buggy hitched up and ready to go in no time. Actually the stable boy did most of it, shooing me away, claiming I was trying to take his job away.

I just wanted to get going. To get Victoria away from here. To spend time alone with her without having to worry about what other people thought. Without her sister watching our every move.

Without having to worry about the whole time travel dilemma.

I didn't care if she was from the future or the county next door. I just liked spending time with her. Looking at her. Talking with her

I might as well give up on fooling myself about that. I wanted to court her.

It might take a minute for me to get around the fact that my siblings had married her siblings, but I would work my way around it.

The more time I spent with her, the easier it was to not think about all that, much less worry about it.

I jumped down from the buggy and secured the horse to the

hitching post before dashing up the steps toward the front door. Victoria should be ready to go by now.

Villars opened the door as I reached for the knob.

"Good day," Villars said with a nod.

"Good morning, Villars." I stepped inside and Villars closed the door behind me.

"Has Victoria come down yet?" I asked, straightening my cravat. Villars was acting like I didn't live here. Maybe he was becoming a bit addled with age.

"Not yet, I'm afraid," he said. "Would you like to wait in the parlor or the library?"

"I can just wait here," I said. Surely she would be down shortly and we could get going.

"Very well," Villars said, turning to go about his business. But then he stopped.

"It's a good day for a storm," he said over his shoulder, then kept walking.

It was an odd thing to say. It should have meant nothing. Just an addled old man rambling about the weather. Maybe his joints hurt.

But it chilled me to the core.

The storms had something to do with time travel. The time travel almost always seemed to happen when there was a storm.

I stepped into the parlor, in spite of my insistence that I wait in the foyer, and shoved the green velvet curtains aside to look out. It was a perfectly beautiful day. I saw no sign of a storm.

I thought seriously about following Villars. Demanding an explanation.

But that would put me in a desperate light. One I did not care to be in.

I paced back to the foyer. Stared at the clock for a few minutes.

Reminded myself that women took a long time to get ready to go anywhere. It was a universal truth that I doubted changed even over hundreds of years.

In fact, if it did change… if women stopped caring about their appearance, then I was grateful that I lived in the time period I was in.

I watched the steady ticking of the grandfather clock. Listened to the day-to-day activities of the house.

Aunt Eloise was back in the kitchen talking with someone. I couldn't understand her words, but she didn't sound happy. Nothing unusual. I wasn't sure I'd ever heard her sound happy.

The clang of metal from the blacksmith drifted through the open window along with the mournful wail of the steamboat horn.

I walked back to the parlor. Stood in front of the piano, silent now. When I tapped one of the keys, the light sound hung in the air for all to hear.

I stepped away from the piano, feeling like I'd intruded on something I shouldn't have and walked back to the foyer.

Mackenzie appeared at the top of the stairs, worry gathered at her brow.

"Is Victoria down here?" she asked.

"No." I stepped forward. "She isn't up there?"

Mackenzie shook her head.

I took the steps two at the time, quickly reaching the second floor.

"You looked in her room?"

"Of course," she said, keeping up with me as I raced down the hallway.

I threw open Victoria's door and a quick glance confirmed what Mackenzie had already told me.

I turned and faced Mackenzie.

"You didn't see… anything?"

Mackenzie lowered her gaze and shook her head.

"I went into my room to get some ribbons." She held up a ball of blue ribbons I hadn't noticed until now.

"What do you think?" I asked, going to the balcony door and looking outside even though I already knew she wasn't out there.

Mackenzie looked at me with moisture in her eyes.

"She went home."

I stepped past her. Paced over to the vanity.

I bent over and picked up one white satin shoe.

27

VICTORIA

Home.

I stood at the top of the stairs. Lightning and thunder swirled all around me.

The house smelled stale replacing the clean scent of magnolias.

And it was quiet. Just the distant steady hum of the central air conditioning behind the

blowing rain and the deafening thunder.

No people to give it life. No music.

No clock ticking.

I took a step, surprised by the swishing of my dress.

Mackenzie had picked out a light blue dress with some splashes of green and pink for me to wear. It was a beautiful dress held out by wide bell-shaped hoops.

But even more, I realized I was only wearing one shoe.

Holding onto the banister, I pulled the shoe off my foot. One white satin shoe.

Just like Cinderella.

I lifted the skirts ever so elegantly and started down the stairs.

It was quiet in the house. So lonely.

The house was dark, lit only by the flash of lightning.

As I went down stairs, I ran everything I needed to do through my head.

Check my phone messages.

I froze three steps from the first floor.

Kit Kat.

Still holding the shoe, I hit the first floor and ran toward the kitchen. The empty food bowl sat next to a water bowl with barely any water. But no cat.

For someone who was always so calm in the face of emergency, I felt panicky.

How long had I been gone?

With lightning flashing and thunder rumbling all around me, I went back toward the foyer.

Kit Kat had to be here somewhere. He just had to be.

I went into the parlor and looked around.

Then I saw him.

Curled up on the sofa.

He lifted his head and looked at me.

He backed up as I ran toward him and knelt down, dropping the shoe.

"It's okay," I said. "It's me. I'm so sorry."

I gathered him up into my arms. He was so fragile.

How long had he been without food?

I carried him back to the kitchen and sat him on the floor.

Relief washed through me when he stood up and looked at me.

When he walked to the empty food bowl and looked back up at me, my heart broke.

I grabbed the bag of cat food and filled his bowl. While I was still pouring the kibbles, he stuck his head into the bowl and started to eat.

I felt his stomach, but he didn't seem noticeably thin.

Taking a can of food from the pantry, I poured it out on a saucer and set it down next to him. He moved from the dry kibbles to eat the canned food.

I filled the water bowl and knelt next to him while he ate.

I sat back on my heels, the blue dress spilling all around me and wiped the moisture from my eyes.

28

GRANT

For the next four days after Victoria vanished, presumably back to her own time, I paced the house like an angry caged bear.

Everyone stopped speaking to me. I barely ate. I drank too much.

After two days, I was sick of whiskey and only ate what Villars left at my door.

What I did manage to eat, I didn't taste.

This morning I sat outside on the balcony, holding the little white slipper.

No one could explain to me why this had happened.

Not Sophia. Not Mackenzie. Not even Cameron who had shown up on his own accord. Maybe he had sensed something going on with his sister because no one had gotten a message to him that Victoria was here. I certainly hadn't.

The beautiful white magnolias in the garden below tormented me with their sweet scent that reminded me of Victoria.

Everything reminded me of her.

Four days had passed and not once had I ridden out to look over the plants in my field.

It was time.

It was time to pull myself together and get back to business.

Victoria was gone, leaving nothing but her memory and a white shoe to torment me.

With a muttered oath, I got up and went inside. Tossed the shoe onto the bed.

I changed into my riding clothes and went outside to saddle up Fair Flax.

Even the horse seemed surprised to see me.

As I rode out to my measly two acres of land, I wondered how I had gotten here.

I'd gone from wanting very little to do with ladies to being tormented and lovestruck.

That's what I was. Lovestruck.

Damn it.

It's what I deserved for not courting a variety of women like a normal man.

No. I had to wait for that perfect girl.

Too bad that perfect girl had to be from another time.

It was fitting, though, I mused, since my siblings had all married Becquerels from the future.

I would have married Victoria if she'd stayed.

Sophia and Mackenzie had tried to tell me that she would come back. If she could. Then they would look at each other and I knew that they did not believe their own words. The words they were saying to ease my pain.

I'd heard them talking about how Victoria was firmly grounded in her world. A doctor with a busy life. They could not see her ever giving that up.

She had not visited her Grandpa since she was fifteen.

Fifteen. The same age I had been when I'd seen Victoria in the mist.

Although I had no grounds to base my belief, I knew it had been her.

My heart told me it had been her.

That I had waited for her all these years.

Sitting at the top of the knoll overlooking the river—the same spot I'd thought to build a house for me and Victoria—I watched a steamboat make its way up the Mississippi River. Listened to its mournful horn. And knew that I would never stop waiting for her.

Even if it meant waiting the rest of my life.

29

VICTORIA

I stood in front of the grandfather clock, staring at the silent dial, the little glass door open.

I cautiously placed a finger on the key.

The key that *could* though not necessarily *would* send a person through time.

I had a good memory. I remembered exactly what Mackenzie had told me.

Put the key in the clock. Then in the second between the lightning flash and following thunder, turn the clock back one hour.

It was a formula. I was good at formulas.

I had the clock. I had the key.

What I did not have was the storm.

According to my phone, I had been in the past for three days. That told me that the time travel was not linear. Time spent in the past did not correspond with time in the present.

After changing into blue jeans and a long-sleeve t-shirt, I'd gotten a lot done today. The first thing I had done was to send Tracie a text asking her to please come out to check on Kit Kat in two days unless she heard from me. I'd put out all the food he had, filling up three large bowls and I'd ordered some more to be delivered tomorrow. I'd also filled up three large bowls with water.

I'd called to check on Grandpa. His rehab had gone well and he was scheduled to be released early.

The way I figured it, even if Tracie did not come out, Kit Kat could survive until Grandpa got home.

If something happened to me.

And, it seemed, I was preparing for that possibility.

I called my hospital and cancelled all my appointments until further notice.

I wasn't leaving here until I seriously got some things figured out.

After closing the glass door on the clock, I went outside and sat in a rocking chair on the veranda.

The swing where I had sat with Grant was gone. And although I looked, I saw no sign of where it had been. The ceiling boards must have replaced. Repainted. Over the last couple hundred years.

As I rocked gently in the chair, I studied the oak trees.

The magnificently large moss-covered oak trees with branches that dipped down so low they nearly touched the ground.

And I sat there watching blue birds searching for food on the overgrown lawn, I made the definitive decision that I had indeed gone back into the past.

There was no other explanation.

I sat there, something I had not done since I was fifteen years old and did nothing except watch the sun set.

After that day, at age fifteen, when I had taken an aimless walk beneath the oak trees and encountered a boy in the mist, I had kept myself busy. That fall I started taking college classes in addition to my regular classes. Then college. Then medical school. Then work.

I kept my head down and never dealt with what I had seen that day.

Cars with loud mufflers passed by on the road. Barges traveled up and down the river. Everything went on as usual.

Life went on as usual.

But my life had changed.

My life would never be the same.

As darkness settled in, I went inside, locked the door, and turned on the Weather Channel.

Kit Kat jumped onto the sofa and, curling up against me, went to sleep.

I opened a box of letters that Grandpa had saved and read late into the night.

30

GRANT

Two weeks later I rode Fair Flax along the river road on my way home from town. Today had been a good day. Today I had finalized an investment in a twenty-acre tract of land not far from the two-acre property my father had deeded to me.

After the paperwork was complete, the attorney had asked me to go to his house. To meet his wife and have a drink with him to celebrate. His father was friends with my uncle, so I guess he wanted to establish a friendship with me.

It probably would have been a good business move. If I was going to live here and be successful, I needed friends. People I could trust both personally and in business.

But I'd come up with an excuse. Something about my uncle needing me. Really I just wanted to get home.

I was something of a recluse by nature anyway, but since Victoria had come here, disrupted my life, then disappeared, I was even more reclusive than before.

I would have to do something about that. I knew it.

But what I really wanted to do was to wait. To wait until I had Victoria with me.

With her by my side, I wouldn't mind social engagements. In fact, I would probably enjoy them.

Still. Today I had made a big step. I was always thinking forward. Preparing for the day when Victoria returned.

When—I refused to think *if*—she returned, the first thing I would have to do was to convince her to let me court her.

I had little experience in actual courtship. Most of what I knew about courtship came from watching my brothers. And some of the things they had done over the years was just plain stupid.

I was no saint, by any means, but out of all my brothers, I was the serious one. I didn't mind that reputation. It reflected my natural inclinations.

There was a storm brewing off in the south, so I nudged Fair Flax into a gallop.

I went straight to the barn, slid off his back, and went to work on brushing him down.

Andrew rode in a few minutes later.

"There you are," he said. "Where have you been?"

"I had some business in town," I said, glancing up at my brother. "Looks like we both barely missed getting caught in the storm."

"Yeah, well." Andrew slid off the horse. "I was actually out looking for you."

"For me?" My hands froze and I looked at my brother. "Why? What's happened?"

"Nothing really serious," he said. "At least not for us. More curious actually."

I ran the brush down Fair Flax's neck and Andrew picked up a brush of his own.

We worked in silence for a few minutes.

"Are you going to tell me?" I asked him.

"Trying to decide."

"Somehow this isn't making me feel any better. Is someone hurt or sick?"

Andrew stopped and looked in the general direction of the house.

"Emma is back."

Emma was Uncle Samuel and Aunt Eloise's daughter. She'd been gone to boarding school for several months now.

"Okay," I said. "What's curious about that?"

"She just showed up," he said.

"I'm still not seeing a problem. Unless it's going to involve piano recitals."

"Good God. I hope not." Andrew shuddered. "But I will confess that it's the first thing I thought of, too, when I saw her."

Aunt Eloise had notoriously forced anyone who happened to be around to sit for hours listening to her daughter play the piano.

Andrew and I had both had our fair share of that torture. Unfortunately, Emma had no talent and very little skill at the piano. Andrew referred to those sessions as watching paint drying.

"I don't think you understand," Andrew said. "No one went to town to pick her up and no one saw her arrive."

"What are you saying?" I asked. This was not what I was hoping for. I was hoping for Victoria to arrive out of the blue. Not Emma.

Andrew lowered his voice. "We—Mackenzie and I—think she's come from another time."

"What the—"

Andrew shrugged. "I guess Uncle Samuel carries the blood of the spell. She could have… acquired it through him."

"I guess," I said. "So. She wasn't at boarding school."

"No one's talking," Andrew shrugged.

"Well hell."

What was wrong with the fates of time? Victoria should be the one traveling here.

I just hoped there wasn't a limit on time travel tickets.

31

VICTORIA

I woke to the crash of thunder and the flash of lightning.

I'd fallen asleep on the sofa.

Sitting up, I worked on orienting myself.

There had been no storm in the forecast. I'd had the Weather Channel on all evening. In fact, it was still on. And there it was. A band of storms coming right through.

I needed to think.

I hadn't decided for sure what I wanted to do.

But now was the time.

Now was the moment I needed to have a decision made and ready to implement.

I wasn't dressed for the past. I was wearing jeans and a long-sleeved t-shirt. I had a perfectly good dress upstairs in my room, but it would take time to go upstairs and change.

It didn't matter anyway. Everyone in the past knew I was from the future.

I picked up Kit Kat. Held him close to me as a bolt of lightning shot through the window followed by a crash of thunder.

"What do I do Kit Kat?"

As the storm raged all around me, it occurred to me that I had already decided.

Why else would I still be here? Why else would I have cancelled all my appointments until further notice?

This was the longest I had gone without working. Ever.

I blew out a breath.

And I knew. I had already decided.

I set Kit Kat aside.

With the storm raging all around, this was it.

It was time.

I went to the foyer to stand in front of the clock.

My hand shook as I opened the little glass door.

Kit Kat wound his way around my legs. I didn't have to worry about him. He had plenty of food and water. Tracie would be coming out to feed him again in two days.

Lighting flashed through the landing window. Was that close enough?

Kit Kat stood up, putting his front paws on my legs, startling me.

The thunder rumbled before I could touch the clock's minute hand.

Kit Kat meowed, standing up on his hind legs, patting my right knee.

"What?" I reached down an picked him up. He was purring now.

A bolt of lightning flashed through the front door.

I gasped.

My hands trembling, I pressed a finger against the minute hand and carefully twirled it back one hour.

Then thunder shook the house itself and the electricity went out.

I steadied myself against the clock, my fingers grasping at anything.

I stood perfectly still, my ears ringing from the thunder. Then I heard the faint, but steady ticking of the clock.

I jumped when it began to toll the hour.

The broken clock tolling the hour!

Then I heard piano music.

Very bad piano music.

32

GRANT

Wherever Emma had been, she had not learned to play the piano any better. In fact, if anything, she had gotten worse.

Perhaps Aunt Eloise should have given her some time to rest before insisting that she sit at the piano.

Fortunately, Aunt Eloise had not required us to sit in the parlor while she played.

The women were in there working on their needlepoint, but Andrew and I stood outside on the veranda, polluting the fresh air with cigars.

"This is a good one," I said. "You did well."

"I agree." Andrew took a puff and blew out a trio of smoke rings. I never had mastered that dubious skill. I wasn't that interested in tobacco and I rarely smoked, but this was a big deal to Andrew. He was investing his future fortune into it.

"Have you made any more progress on your house?" I asked.

"It's slowed down," he said. "I'm spending a lot of time with Mackenzie."

"As you should," I said, determined to keep any trace of envy out of my voice.

And I wasn't really envious. I was just impatient to get my own family started.

"How did you stand the waiting?" I asked. "For Mackenzie?" I remembered he had waited over a year.

Andrew blew out a breath and shook his head.

"I didn't stand it."

I understood. He merely tolerated it.

"I threw myself into building our house. Just bided my time."

Just bided his time.

"I need a whiskey," I said, pushing away from the railing. "You want one?"

"Absolutely," he said.

"Wait here," I said. "I'll get it."

I looked for a place to set my cigar, then just gave up and handed it to Andrew.

He chuckled and took it from me.

"Don't get lost," he said. "I need something to dull Emma's music."

"She needs to take a break and let Mackenzie play," I said, over my shoulder.

"You go ahead and tell Aunt Eloise that," he said.

I laughed and went inside the house.

Just as I stepped inside, the music stopped abruptly, leaving a discordant echo in the air.

Emma never ended a song like that.

Following my instinct, I bypassed the library where the best whiskey was kept and kept walking to the foyer.

A young lady with long brunette hair stood facing the grandfather clock as it chimed the hour.

It was Victoria.

She was dressed in pants and she was holding something.

A cat.

Victoria was holding a cat.

33

VICTORIA

The echo of the clock's chimes hung in the air, along with the discordant jumble of piano keys after whoever had been played dropped their hands on the keys.

Growing up with Mackenzie playing the piano ALL the time, I was well familiar with all possible piano sounds.

Clutching Kit Kat to my chest, I turned slowly toward the sounds of the piano.

"Victoria!" Mackenzie, wearing an emerald dress with a long, full skirt, was rushing toward me. She hugged me, then backed up.

"Oh my God," she said. "Kit Kat."

I just stood there, stunned as she took the cat out of my arms.

I had just traveled back in time. AND I had brought Kit Kat with me.

"You brought Grandpa's cat?!"

I shook my head.

My ears were buzzing and I felt a little bit off-balance. But I looked past her. Looking… Looking for Grant.

"How did this happen?" Mackenzie asked, searching my eyes as she hugged the cat.

"I don't know." I put a hand on my forehead. But I did know. "It worked," I said, looking back at her.

"What worked?"

"The formula," I said. "I used the formula and it worked."

"Come," she said, tugging my arm. "Come sit down."

She led me into the parlor and guided me to the sofa.

The girl who'd been playing the piano, sat watching us, her chin on her hands. She was probably late teens. Sixteen years old maybe. She wore a pale-yellow dress that complimented her long blonde hair. She was quite pretty. It was unfortunate that she had no skill in playing the piano.

There was no one else in the room.

"How did this happen?" Mackenzie said, nodding at the cat, then sitting next to me and arranging her skirts around her.

My head was starting to clear a bit.

"I think he wanted to come with me," I said.

"Is Grandpa still in the hospital?" Mackenzie asked, looking a bit perplexed and ignoring my statement.

"Yes," I said, looking around again for Grant. "But—" Then I saw him standing at the parlor door, wearing an unreadable expression.

My heart rate shot into overdrive.

Grant was the reason I had come back here.

I'd wanted to be close to my siblings, sure, but I wouldn't have given up everything in my life without Grant being a factor.

The girl started playing the piano again. She was still playing badly, but I tuned it out. All I could focus on right now was Grant.

He walked straight to me, without hesitation, and knelt in front of me, causing my heart to do summersaults.

He took both my hands in his.

"Hi," he said, the corners of his lips turned up in a smile that reached his eyes.

"Hi," I said, my voice barely audible to my own ears.

He kissed the back of my fingertips.

"Welcome home," he said.

Home.

That's where I was.

"Looks like you brought a friend," he said.

I looked over at Kit Kat. The cat just blinked at me, kneading his paws and, I swear, he was smiling.

"I guess I did."

34

GRANT

I didn't even care right now that Emma was playing the piano, hitting wrong notes that were painful to listen to.

All I cared about was that I had Victoria back, her hands in mind.

"Is Grandpa, okay?" Mackenzie asked.

I didn't even care that I had to share her with Mackenzie, at least for the moment.

"Yes," Victoria said, shifting her gaze to her sister. "He's doing well and looks like he'll be going home early."

"That's wonderful news."

Kit Kat left Mackenzie's lap and stumbled over to snuggle up in Victoria's.

"Did you mean to bring Grandpa's cat?" Mackenzie asked.

"No," she said, her gaze back on mine again. "It was Kit Kat's idea."

Mackenzie didn't ask for further explanation.

"We have to get a message to him," Mackenzie said. "So he won't worry about Kit Kat."

"A message? How are we going to do that?"

Andrew came to the door and took in the situation.

"You're back," he said, coming to sit on the arm of the chair next to Mackenzie.

"Hello Andrew," Victoria said.

The music was starting to wear on me now. I was so used to hearing Mackenzie play that it was painful listening to someone who had little skill.

"Can we go outside?" I asked. "I think some fresh air would do us good."

"Yes," Victoria said, handing the cat back to Mackenzie.

I helped Victoria to her feet, tucked her hand in the crook of my elbow, and led her outside into the cool fresh air.

I held the swing while she sat down, then sat down beside her.

"I didn't know that cats could travel through time," I said.

"I didn't either. But it's not such a stretch since I was holding him."

"Seems like everybody brings something with them."

"Like what?" she asked.

"Like books on a screen."

She grinned. "I didn't think about doing that."

"I'm just glad you're here," I said.

"Me too." She smiled up at me.

"I knew you would come back," I said.

"Is that so? How did you know that?"

I looked out over the gardens, lightning bugs twinkling among the flowers.

That was a good question. How did I know?

"You had to," I said.

"That's a rather vague answer," she said.

Clouds shifted over the moon, leaving it dark.

I wasn't sure she was ready for the truth.

I wasn't sure I was ready for the truth.

But she was looking for an answer.

"I knew because..." I lightly ran my fingers along her chin and her eyes drifted closed.

"I knew because I couldn't live without you."

Then I leaned forward and pressed my lips against hers.

Something I had been waiting for what seemed like a lifetime to do.

And nothing had ever felt so right.

I pulled back and she looked up at me with clear eyes.

"I have a feeling that isn't customary," she said with a little smile playing about her lips.

"I this case," I said, grinning. "I think it is."

Then I kissed her again.

35

VICTORIA

The next afternoon, I knelt in the floor of the guest room with my sisters Mackenzie and Sophia.

When Sophia opened a shoe box and pulled out some paper and a modern ink pen, Kit Kat climbed into the little box and curled up.

"Mackenzie is right," Sophia said. "We have to let Grandpa know that you're here and that you brought Kit Kat with you."

"It wasn't my idea to bring him," I said.

"It's okay," Mackenzie said, scratching Kit Kat's head. "I missed the little guy."

"And so will Grandpa," Sophia said. "Kit Kat is all he has for company."

I shook my head. "He actually has Tracie now."

"Who's Tracie?" Sophia asked, smoothing out a piece of the paper and preparing to write on it.

"She's Grandpa's caregiver," Mackenzie said. "His companion."

"Oh," Sophia said. "I did not know that."

"Actually Cameron started the whole process," I said. "So how are we going to get a message to Grandpa?"

"It's really cool." Sophia grinned.

"She only says that because it was her idea," Mackenzie said. "being an architect and all."

"We write the letter," Sophia said, ignoring us. "Then we put it behind this window frame right here. Grandpa pries the frame off and there's a letter."

"The paper doesn't rot?" I ran a hand over the paper.

"It's alkaline paper," Mackenzie said. "It lasts for centuries."

"So this is like a mailbox." I ran my hand over the window frame.

I looked over Sophia's shoulder as she started to write.

Dear Grandpa,

I hope you are feeling better. We're all here. Safely in 1854.

She sat back and shoved her hair out of her face while Mackenzie and I waited.

"I really miss him," Sophia said, blinking back unshed tears.

"We all do," I said, putting an arm around her shoulders. "But he's okay."

"I know." She wiped at her eyes and lifted her chin.

Victoria just got here. And she brought Kit Kat with her.

"I feel really bad about it," I said, sitting back.

"You said he wanted to come," Mackenzie said. "Maybe he's supposed to be here. With us."

"Maybe," I said. But I still felt bad. Maybe he had just been afraid of the storm.

Sophia kept writing.

. . .

Victoria has a beau.

"A beau," I said, trying not to laugh.

"A boyfriend," Sophia explained.

"I know what a beau is. But..."

Both Sophia and Mackenzie looked at me with raised eyebrows.

"He's the reason you came back, right?" Mackenzie asked, with a glance at Sophia.

I pressed my fingers against my brow. "Is it that obvious?"

"Only to us," Sophia said. "Because we did the same thing. We came back here for our men. And Cameron came back here for Isabella."

"Why?" I asked, mostly to myself, looking outside at the oak trees that were smaller than they should be.

"It's the spell that saved Vaughn's life," Sophia said.

"How do you feel about it?" Mackenzie asked.

I turned to my sister and laughed.

"Always the psychologist?"

"I can't help it." Mackenzie shrugged. "If someone got a fever. Wouldn't you try to help them?"

"Of course," I said. But I honestly had not thought that far ahead. I had put all my eggs in one basket, so to speak. And that basket was Grant.

"Does it always work out?" I asked.

"Nothing's definite," Mackenzie said.

"Of course not," Sophia said. "The only reason the time travel happens is so people can be with their soul mates."

Soul mates. I had not considered that either.

I took a deep breath.

We all signed our names to the letter, expressing our love

for Grandpa. Then Sophia carefully used a pry bar to pry up the window pane just enough to place the letter beneath it.

"I have to be careful," she said. "If I do this too often and damage the window pane, someone in between us and Grandpa might decide to fix it and find our letters."

"I just wish we could hear back from Grandpa somehow," Mackenzie said.

"We all do," I said.

I especially felt bad since I was one who had stolen his cat.

As though he sensed my distress, Kit Kat came over to me and head bumped me.

"He seems happy," Mackenzie said.

"We have to figure out what to feed him," I said.

I'd brought him, so I was responsible for taking care of him.

"Okay," Sophia said. "That's done. Let's go see what our men are doing."

Our men.

I rather liked the sound of that.

And I certainly was looking forward to kissing my particular man again.

As much as I was reluctant to admit it, Sophia was probably right about the whole soul mates thing.

36

GRANT

With renewed optimism, I rode out to my fields early the next morning.

The cotton plants were growing heartily. Soon they would be knee high.

At the top of the knoll, I slid off Fair Flax and walked around a bit, loosely holding the reins.

It was a gentle slope from the edge of my planted rows of cotton down to the edge of the Mississippi.

Yes, I decided. This was going to be a good place for a house.

I'd bring Victoria out first, though, and make sure she liked it, too.

I wanted her to be happy above all else. From listening to her sisters, I got the sense that ladies in the future pretty much ran things. Or at the least were equal to men.

I actually liked the idea. I'd always thought women should be more involved in business decisions. And on top of all that, Victoria was a physician, so she was educated.

Whistling to myself, I sat on the ground and watched a steamboat full of people pass by on the river.

I waved and was pretty sure I saw someone wave back.

After we were married, Victoria and I could travel to New Orleans. Maybe go there for our honeymoon.

I could show her where I grew up.

Suddenly ready to get back, I mounted Fair Flax and nudged him back in the direction toward home. She should be waking up soon.

I was getting ahead of myself again.

I had to keep reminding myself that courting came before marriage.

But there were always exceptions to every rule and considering that Victoria was from the future, I was pretty sure customary rules could be broken with her.

At the sound of a rider headed my way, I stopped.

It was Andrew, his dog Biscuit at his heels.

"What is it?" I asked as he came to a stop next to me. I could tell by his expression that something was wrong. My first thought was that Victoria must have gone through time again.

"It's Father," he said. "He's taken ill."

Father.

"What illness?" I asked. I tried to remember when I had last seen Father. Yesterday? The day before? How long had he been ill?

"I don't know," Andrew said. "Mother won't let me near their room."

"What are his symptoms?" I asked.

"They only told me has a fever."

A fever.

It was too early in the season for yellow fever. Wasn't it? And we were too far north.

Mother and Father had brought us north to the Natchez area every year specifically to avoid any of us coming down with it. Father's parents had both died from the yellow fever before I was even born.

"Did someone send for the doctor?" I asked as we both took off, galloping toward the house.

"Yes," Andrew said, then we rode the rest of the way toward the house in silence.

We dropped our horses off at the barn with a lick and a promise, then headed into the house. A cloud of dread swirling around us.

Neither one of us would say it, but I was certain we were both thinking it.

Yellow fever.

37

VICTORIA

There was a definite cloud hanging over the household.

I felt it even as I came downstairs after getting dressed. Mackenzie had picked out a pale green silk gown for me to wear today. She said it brought out the green in my eyes.

As I passed through the foyer with the steadily ticking grandfather clock, I felt it.

I went straight into the kitchen for coffee, but no one was there. There was a coffee pot and cups on the table along with some fruit.

I poured coffee, black and inky looking into a cup, took one sip and wrinkled my nose.

Picking up a handful of fresh strawberries, I took them and my cup out onto the veranda.

Since I had a serious caffeine addiction from working long hours at the hospital, I was going to have to suck it up and drink some of the coffee or put up with three days of headaches and irritability.

I knew. I'd tried it before.

I sat on one of the white wooden rockers and ate the strawberries before tackling the coffee.

Yesterday had been a day of pleasant day reunion with my siblings. I'd gotten to know their spouses. Isabella, Nathan, and Andrew. All good people. And they all seemed happily married. But as such, I hadn't had much if any time alone with Grant.

But today that should be different.

Cameron and Isabella were planning to head back into town where they had a townhouse. I was so proud of Cameron. He was channeling his screenwriting skills into writing novels. He was a fast writer and was quickly becoming in demand for the regular dime novels.

According to Sophia, who had done more research on this time period than any of us, the dime novel writers were quite successful. It suited my Maserati driving brother.

I sipped the coffee, then swallowed it down like I would medicine.

With the bitter taste still in my mouth, I looked up to see Andrew and Grant striding purposely from the stables. It was obvious from the way they walked that they were brothers. Yet there were subtle differences. Andrew had a slightly bouncier step whereas Grant had the more serious stride of the oldest brother.

As they came closer, I saw that both of them wore worried expressions.

Setting my coffee cup aside, I went to the banister and waited. The swish of my skirts was still a novelty and I wondered if I would ever get used to wearing skirts after spending years wearing hardly anything other than scrubs.

The wind tossed my hair across my face and I pulled it over my left shoulder.

When they reached the top of the stairs, Grant took my hands in his and kissed my cheek while Andrew waited.

"Has something happened?" I asked.

"It's Father," he said. "He's taken a fever."

"A fever." That explained the cloud I'd sensed over the household today. I must have been the last one to get up and about this morning.

"How high is it?" I asked, then bit my tongue. He would have no way of knowing without a thermometer.

"I don't know," he said. "I'm on my way to see him now."

"I'll come with you," I said.

"No. If it's the fever, I don't want you catching it."

I nodded and let him go. There was little else I could do at the moment.

But if his father had yellow fever, then it wasn't possible for me or anyone else to catch it from him.

It if was yellow fever, they were going to have to use the mosquito netting I'd seen around some of the beds and not just at night. Mosquitoes bit during the day, too.

I went inside to see if I could find Mackenzie. Being part of the family, she would know more about what was going on. She would also understand when I told her that yellow fever couldn't be transmitted from one person to another.

I went into the library and dropped into an armchair to wait.

It seemed things were complicated no matter what time period it was.

There was always something going on.

I blew out a breath. Unfortunately, this family didn't trust me enough to help them yet. Even though Mackenzie had mentioned that I was a doctor, I don't think they remembered. Or maybe it just hadn't sank in.

This was the 1800s, after all. Women weren't supposed to be as educated as me and my sisters.

38

GRANT

I paced the upstairs hallway, waiting for the doctor to come out from father's room with news.

I'd left Victoria was downstairs with the other women.

My sister Isabella wasn't about to leave with our father sick like this. Even now she sat at the end of the hallway. Her hands busy with needlepoint. Not talking to anyone. That was how she coped with worry.

I paced quietly, not talking to anyone. Isabella sat quietly, keeping her hands busy, also not talking to anyone. We were alike in that way.

Andrew was out back with Mackenzie distracting themselves with a game of croquette. I didn't understand how he could to that, but it was his way.

Nathan wasn't here yet. He and Sophia were busy with their daughter.

Mother, in spite of the dangers of the illness, was in the room with Father and the doctor. Doc White.

As the clock chimed twelve times, Victoria came upstairs with a tray of bread and fruit.

She walked up and stood on her tiptoes to kiss me.

I took the tray from her, set it aside, and pulled her close. It felt so good to hold her close. Maybe this could be my new way of dealing with worry. Holding Victoria.

"Any word yet?" she asked.

"No," I said, the worry rushing back, just thinking about it. "I don't know why it's taking him so long."

"I'm sure he'll be out soon," she said. "I thought you and Isabella might be hungry."

"That's very thoughtful," I said, though I wasn't sure my stomach could tolerate any food right now.

Holding the tray against me with one arm, I took Victoria's hand and we walked over to where Isabella sat.

"I thought you might want something to eat," Victoria said with a little smile.

Isabella looked up from her needlepoint. "Thank you," she said. "That's very thoughtful." But she went right back to her needlepoint.

"May I sit with you for a moment?" Victoria asked.

Isabella shrugged. "Of course."

After Victoria sat, I picked up a piece of bread and ignored the way it had no taste and then sat like a rock in the pit of my stomach.

I knew better than to eat when I was overcome with worry, but I wanted Victoria to feel appreciated.

I set the half eaten piece of bread aside.

"I'm afraid I'm beset with worry at the moment," I said.

"I understand," she said. "Please don't feel obligated."

We sat a few minutes in silence, the only sound the soft tap of Isabella's needles.

Victoria cleared her throat.

"You know what?" she said. "I think I'll just go check to see what's going on in there. Maybe I can help."

"Before I could stop her, she was up and making her way to Father's door. With a helpless glance at Isabella, I got up to follow her, but it was too late.

39

VICTORIA

I burst into the bedroom door without knocking.

Knowing I was breaking all kinds of protocol, I decided I may as well break it all the way. The room was dark and stuffy. The windows were closed and drapes pulled to block out any sunlight.

Mr. Laurent lay in the bed beneath a blanket, his eyes closed. His wife sitting on one side of him, the doctor on the other.

"Excuse me," I said. "I apologize for barging in like this, but this is not helping him."

Going to the window, I through open the drapes and pushed open the window.

Mrs. Laurent gasped at the onslaught of fresh air and sunshine.

"What's the meaning of this?" Doc White asked.

Grant stood in the doorway now.

"I can help him," I said, feeling like first year resident all over again.

Grant crossed the room to stand next to me.

"Victoria is a doctor," he said.

I appreciated his support, but I had more than a feeling it wasn't going to sway anyone in this room.

The doctor stood up. "That's all well and good. But Mr. Laurent is under my care. You'll close that window at once."

I shook my head.

"I can't do that," I said. "it would do more harm than good."

"Who is this woman?" Doc White asked, looking around at no one in particular.

Grant took my arm and tucked my hand in the crook of his elbow.

"This is my fiancé," he said. "and I trust her with my father's life."

Mrs. Laurent put a hand over her mouth.

"Well then," Doc White said, picked up his hat, and jammed it on his head. "In that case, I'll be on my way."

Grant released my arm and went to open the bedroom door.

The doctor cast one last scathing glance back at me, before taking his leave. Grant closed the door behind him, then looked from me to his mother and back again.

I steeled myself as Mrs. Laurent got up and came toward me.

A glance out of the corner of my eye told me that Grant didn't know what was about to happen either.

Mrs. Laurent took my hands.

"Thank you, Dear," she said. "The doctor wouldn't listen to a thing I tried to tell him. I tried to tell him that Mr. Laurent's parents passed from yellow fever, that I knew what the fever looks like, but he wouldn't listen to a word I was telling him. He insisted that it was too early in the year for the fever."

"It has nothing to do with the time of year," I said with relief that she wasn't angry or offended. "It's spread through mosquitoes."

I looked at Grant. "Yellow fever, if that's what it is, can't be spread from one person to another."

"Good heavens," Mrs. Laurent said, going back to her husband's side. "Are you saying he got it from mosquitoes?"

"If that's what it is, yes," I said. "Do you mind if I take a look?"

"Please," Grant said. "Go ahead.

I placed a hand against Mr. Laurent's forehead and gauged that he had about one hundred one fever.

"Does he have any other symptoms?" I asked.

"Headache," Mrs. Laurent said. "Sick to his stomach and exhausted."

I nodded. Typical symptoms, but it was too early to tell. It could be a lot of things.

One thing I was certain of, though. We did not want it to be yellow fever. There's no cure for yellow fever.

40

GRANT

I sat with Father through the night. He mostly slept, but at Victoria's suggestion, I made sure he had plenty of fresh water in case he woke up and when he had chills, I kept the blankets off him. It went against everything I'd ever been taught, but she said the fever needed to be able to come out of his body. I also kept a cool cloth on his forehead when the fever was high.

It made sense that he needed fresh air from an open window, but I draped the mosquito netting around us, too.

I was terrified about my father being ill, worried that I would do something wrong, but I trusted Victoria.

I would have trusted her even if she hadn't been a doctor, simply because she was from the future. People would naturally learn more about treating illnesses as time went by.

I was proud of her for standing up to Doc White for what she believed was best for my father. Even Mother had been grateful.

But there was one matter that I hadn't quite figured out what to do about yet.

I'd introduced her as my fiancé.

I hadn't even begun to court her yet, much less propose. Hell, I hadn't even had the chance to talk to her about it. To explain myself. The truth was, though, I didn't know what to think about it. I didn't know why I had said it except that I'd wanted to show support for her trying to help Father.

She hadn't shown any reaction when I'd said it and I didn't know what to think about that either.

I rinsed out the cloth and placed it back on Father's forehead.

The moon was behind the clouds, the candle providing the only light, meager as it was, in the room.

"Son," Father said, startling me.

"Father." Thank God. "You're awake. How do you feel?"

"I've felt better," he said, his voice barely loud enough for me to hear. "And possibly worse."

"You've been very sick," I said, moving the candle closer.

"I know."

I filled a glass with water and held it to his lips. It chilled my heart to see my strong father like this. He'd always been so healthy. So… alive. It was a cruel reminder that he was getting up in age and wouldn't always be here.

"I need to tell you something," he said, but his eyes drifted closed and I thought he had gone back to sleep.

"That girl," he said after a moment.

"Which girl?" I asked, though Victoria was the only girl in my head.

"Victoria," he said.

I waited and the clock chimed the hour downstairs. One chime. One o'clock. And it sounded very, very far away.

"If you love her, don't let her go."

I shook my head once. Looked at nothing across the room.

"I'm not sure that's up to me," I said.

"I think it's more up to you than you think."

"How so?" I asked, looking at my father.

He and I had missed so many opportunities to talk. There were so many things he could have told me and we'd missed so much time.

"Can I get some more water?" he asked.

"Of course." I handed him the cup of water and held it while he drank.

"Thank you," he said, then rested a moment.

I rinsed out the cloth and put it back on his head.

I never would have thought I would be the one doing this. But my mother needed to sleep and everyone else had things they needed to do. They had wives. Husbands. Children.

"By all rights," Father said. "your mother should have traveled in time."

"She carries Vaughn's blood," I whispered, the realization sinking in. I knew this, but hearing my father say it made it more definite. More real.

"That's right," Father said.

"But she had you."

Father nodded and closed his eyes again.

"That's right," he said. "We were always meant to be together. There was no one else for either of us. Some would say we're soul mates."

Soul mates. Hearing my father talk about being my mother's soul mate twisted something deep in my heart and made it impossible for me to say anything.

"If she's your soul mate," Father said. "She'll stay here. With you."

"How do I know?" I asked, barely getting the words past my throat.

"You just do, Son," Father said. "You just do."

He was right, of course.

I had known.

I had known since I was fifteen years old.

41

VICTORIA

The next night I sat out on the veranda in the swing next to Grant.

The night was beautiful and smelled like honeysuckle and magnolia. The lightning bugs put on a show for us across the lawn and the frogs and crickets provided the music.

Grant had one arm around me and I rested my head on his chest.

It was so calm. So calm and peaceful.

Such a contrast to my hectic life back in my own time.

I had chosen this. I had chosen to be here. With this man.

I couldn't say why I'd chosen to come back here. The first time had just happened. The fates of time had thrown us together. But the second time had been my choice.

If I was going to live here, I had to find a way to be productive. But I had no hobbies. No skills other than medicine.

I wanted to talk to Grant about it, but I wasn't sure I should just yet.

He'd referred to me as his fiancé to the doctor, but I was fairly certain that had just been situational.

Normally, I would have just asked for clarification, but I was much too aware of the time period I was in.

"Tell me more about what it's like in your world," he said.

My world. Somehow I wasn't thinking of that future as my world so much anymore. All three of my siblings were here. Had made their lives here. Families. My sister Sophia already had one baby and one on the way. My other sister Mackenzie was also expecting a baby.

I didn't know so much what Cameron and Isabella were doing. She was a good match for him. She was less traditional and seemed to want to be more like him. More modern—as modern as one could be during this time.

"It's busy," I said. "There are very few moments like this."

"You mean there's no courting?" he asked.

"No. There's courting. It's called dating. Sort of the same thing."

"So then what do people do during their courtship?"

"All sorts of things."

"Like picnics?"

"No. They eat at… cafés mostly. Or they take food home and eat it."

"Hmm. So if we were in the future—in your time—what would we be doing right now?"

"That's a good question."

I just wasn't so sure how much I wanted to get into explaining things.

"We would probably be watching… listening to music." It would take longer to explain television, so that would have to wait.

"Okay," he said. "That's not so different."

"And we'd be doing something on our cells." I held up a hand. "Don't ask me what a cell is. I'll have to explain it later when we have about a week."

"Is it something similar to Sophia's Kindle?" he asked, kissing me on the cheek.

"Sophia has a Kindle? How?" I leaned up to look at him.

"She charges it with sunlight," he said. "it's an amazing gadget."

"Wow," I said. "I didn't know she did that. She must have been really prepared."

"Unlike you?" Grant said, with a teasing nudge. "You just jumped right in."

"With both feet," I said.

"I'm glad you did."

"Yeah? Have you decided what you're going to do with me yet?"

"Oh, I don't know. I—"

Mackenzie came to the door.

"Grant," she said. "Andrew is looking for you."

"Why?" Grant removed his arm from around me and took my hand. "What's happened?"

"It's your father," she said. "He's taken a turn for the worse."

42

GRANT

After what some would call a slight disagreement, we compromised and left the window cracked about one inch and closed the curtains against the cool night air.

I insisted that the window stay open, based on what Victoria had told me, to let in fresh air. Aunt Eloise, on the other hand, was old school and insisted that the window be closed tight and the curtains closed.

Mother stayed out of it, as did Andrew. So it was me against Aunt Eloise.

Victoria and Mackenzie stayed downstairs, insisting they wanted to stay out of family business.

Finally, at the insistence of her husband, Aunt Eloise went to bed and much of the tension magically dissipated from the room.

With Mother manning the cool cloth, I slipped out to find Victoria.

I found her on the sofa in the parlor with Mackenzie. They were curled up on either side of the sofa with Kit Kat right in the middle of them, leaving me a bit envious.

Victoria stood when I walked through the door.

"How is he?" she asked, speaking quietly so as not to wake Mackenzie.

"He's got a high fever again," I said. "And he threw up bile—nothing in his stomach—and has started coughing."

"Did someone send for the doctor?" she asked.

"They did," I said, sitting on an ottoman at her feet.

"I don't know," she said. "The only way to really know is to run tests and I can't do that here." She scrubbed her hands over her face.

"Maybe he just needs to sleep it off," I said, although my heart was not in the words.

Victoria didn't say anything in response.

At a light knock on the front door, I went to open it.

It was the young boy who had ridden into town to fetch Doc White.

"Did you find him?" I asked.

"Yes Sir," the boy said, shifting from one foot to the other. "But he said we'd have to wait until morning."

Doc would naturally say that. Why would the man interrupt his good night's sleep?

"Thank you," I said. "Get some sleep yourself." And closed the door.

Victoria met me at the door.

"Is he coming?" she asked.

"No." I shook my head. "Maybe in the morning."

I didn't want to tell her that doc probably wasn't going to come after the way Victoria had stood up to him.

Some men just weren't willing to listen to women. It was their loss as far as I was concerned.

"Get some sleep." I said. "Tomorrow promises to be a long day."

She nodded. "I'll just sleep down here with Mackenzie. I'm used to sleeping in odd places."

It was an odd statement, but I'd ask her about it later.

For now, I pulled her against me and lifted her chin. Her eyes fluttered closed as my lips captured hers.

The grandfather clock chimed the hour, wrapping us in a cocoon. A place where time stood still.

And the only thing that mattered was the way our lips melded together.

Each time I kissed her, I fell a little bit more in love with this mysterious woman from the future.

43

VICTORIA

Early the next morning, after breakfast with Sophia and Mackenzie, the three of us moved to the parlor.

Everyone else was upstairs, trying to figure out what to do about Mr. Laurent.

Someone had sent for the doctor, but they weren't sure he was going to show up. Apparently, I had offended him to the point that he refused to come back.

Sophia and Mackenzie sat on the sofa, but I went to stand at the window.

"What can we do?" Sophia asked.

"I don't know," Mackenzie said. "But there has to be something."

"I brought some antibiotics, but I'm out. I used all of them."

"They didn't last long, did they?" Mackenzie said. "I can see why."

"Antibiotics won't cure yellow fever," I said, more to myself than anyone in particular.

Sophia and Mackenzie stopped talking. I turned around and faced them.

"But that doesn't matter," I said. "He doesn't have yellow fever."

I had suspected it all along, but I hadn't been willing to say anything without giving it more time to run its course. It wasn't like I could run tests on him.

"What does he have?" Mackenzie asked.

"I'm not sure without more tests," I said.

"But you do know?" she insisted. "Don't you?"

I took a deep breath. I was going out on a limb here. I wouldn't do it with anyone other than my sisters.

"If I tell you, please don't tell anyone," I said. "Because I can't be sure."

"We know," Sophia said. "So what does he have?"

"Could be malaria," I said. "That's actually my first choice."

"Isn't that the same thing?" Sophia asked.

"Not exactly," Mackenzie said.

"Different mosquitoes," I said, turning back around to face the window.

"So it's not yellow fever, but even if it was there's no treatment."

"And we don't have any medications."

"That's right," I said. "I'd even be willing to try the antibiotics."

"I took the last ones for a UTI," Sophia said.

I whirled around. Mackenzie and I just looked at her.

"What? I had no choice."

"I know," I said. "I'm just thinking that what we're doing here is impossible. Without modern medication, I'm not sure we can survive."

"Actually," Mackenzie said. "I borrowed Sophia's Kindle and I've been reading about different herbal treatments."

"That's helpful," I said. "At least we can sort of know what might work."

"It helps to have Victoria here," Sophia said. "I feel a lot better with her here."

"I agree," Mackenzie said. "She knows a lot about medicine."

"I'm right here," I said.

Andrew came to the door.

"Any word from the doctor?" he asked.

Mackenzie just shook her head.

Andrew looked at me, but didn't say anything.

"How is he?" I asked.

"I think you should come up and take a look at him."

"I don't think they want me up there."

"They do," he said. "They're just too upset to know it."

"Great," I said, but I followed him upstairs anyway.

Now that I was going into physician mode, I felt out of place in this long dress. I needed my scrubs. My familiar outfit that I wore to work every day.

It took my eyes a minute to adjust to the dim light inside the room and the stuffiness was almost overwhelming.

This was quite a difference from the antiseptic scent I was used to in hospital rooms.

"Can we open those curtains?" I asked.

Grant moved to open the curtains, letting light spill into the room.

Mr. Laurent lay beneath a blanket, looking quite pale.

I took a deep breath and moved to sit next to him.

Mrs. Laurent, his wife, looked at me with such hopefulness. I'd seen that hopefulness before. I'd seen it when I had to tell people there was no hope.

Telling someone there was nothing I could do had to be THE worst thing I ever did as a physician.

To say this was going to be a challenge, was an understatement.

If there was ever a reason why I would drop my license and stop practicing medicine, that would be it.

Well. That and moving to a different century.

I looked over my shoulder at Grant.

"Can I talk to you?" I asked.

44

GRANT

I sat at the desk in the library taking notes in a blank journal I'd found in my father's desk.

Victoria sat in the armchair holding Sophia's Kindle. I was impressed by the way she knew how to use what she called an electronic format.

It was a cloudy day, so it had taken absolutely no convincing to get me to stay inside and help her with her research.

Even if it hadn't been cloudy, I still would have done it just to be near her.

Villars had brought us a platter of cheese and fruit, but we'd barely touched it.

I was the designated note taker because I could wield a quill pen better than she could.

She wore a frown between her brows that I longed to smooth out.

Maybe later.

"Okay," she said. "write this down."

"Ready," I said, dipping the end of my quill into the ink pot.

"Cinnamon. Ginger. Turmeric. Orange juice. Apple cider vinegar. Fenugreek seeds."

I got all of them down but the last one.

"What kind of seed?"

"Fenugreek."

"I don't know how to spell that," I said.

"Never mind," she said. "We couldn't find it here if we wanted to. It grows in India."

"I can send for some," I said.

She shook her head.

She didn't say it, but I knew what she didn't say. She didn't say we did not have time.

She knew it. I knew it. everyone knew it.

We were at the end of our rope.

Father wasn't getting any better.

He was only getting worse.

There was nothing any of us could do other than to sit and watch him get weaker and weaker.

If we didn't find a way to help him soon, he wasn't going to get better.

"Surely the doctor will have something he can give him," she said, absently. "Quinine."

She tapped the screen, scowling again. Then she looked up.

"Is there a willow tree around here?"

I shrugged. "I wouldn't know.

"Dogwood?"

"Maybe," I said.

"There are so many," she said. "But there's no empirical evidence that they work."

"We're desperate, aren't we?" I asked, setting the pen aside and leaning back.

She blew out a breath and looked into my eyes.

I could see the answer there. I was right. We were at a desperate point.

"I should go into town," she said. "Find the doctor. Apologize."

"Victoria," I said. "Do you think that there is anything that can be done for him? Truly? At this point?"

"I don't know," she said. "I don't know enough about what options there are in this time."

I went over and knelt in front of her. Took her hands in mine.

"I'm so sorry," she said. "I think it's my fault."

"No," I said. "It's not your fault. Doc White wasn't helping Father. In fact, I honestly think that Father would already be gone if you hadn't stopped him."

She looked away, trying to hide the pain in her eyes.

"Did you know that—"

Mackenzie came to the door, interrupting what I had been about to tell her.

It wasn't important anyway.

"Can I talk to you?" Mackenzie asked Victoria.

I excused myself and went outside to the veranda. I took out a handkerchief and wiped at the ink stains on my hands.

I truly believed that Doc White would have killed Father if left to his own devices. Especially when considering that he was planning to bleed Father using leeches. I'd never understood that. Never would.

45

VICTORIA

Mackenzie sat on the arm of the chair in what would no doubt have been a very unladylike position in this time period.

But we were alone, so it didn't matter. Except for the cat. Kit Kat had followed her in and was curled up asleep on one of the book shelves.

The worry on Mackenzie's face was evident and she didn't try to hide it.

Clouds were gathering outside, reflecting the morose mood inside the house. Everyone was quiet, walking around in hushed tones. Even Emma hadn't touched the piano in days.

"I think we're losing him," Mackenzie said.

"I know," I agreed. As much as I didn't want to agree, I did. "I think he could have been treated, but I ran the doctor off."

"It's not your fault," Mackenzie said. "He wasn't doing Mr. Laurent any good."

"But he could have," I said.

"It's not like you to question yourself."

"It's not like me to do something like this. Something I can't fix."

Mackenzie put a hand on my shoulder.

"Maybe it's not fixable," she said.

"Maybe." But I had a hard time believing that. If only I had some antibiotics, I think he would get better."

Mackenzie shook her head. "I know. But we have to adapt."

I ran a hand through my hair.

"I know how this works," I said. "Grant will blame me. Maybe not right now. But later. Later after he thinks about it, he'll blame me."

"Give him a chance," Mackenzie said. "These are different times. Hard times. In this world, Mr. Laurent is an old man."

"An old man," I scoffed. "He's what? Not even fifty years old. He's young."

"In our world he is. We have access to medicines that we don't have here."

Mackenzie's words told me she was transitioning from thinking of herself as being from the future to being here. I wondered if she even noticed.

But she was right. There were medicines in the future that we did not have here.

I turned off the Kindle to save battery and hugged it to me.

There was so much information on here. So much that Sophia had brought with her. She'd also brought antibiotics and she had used them to treat a couple of things that had come up.

Again, I wondered how people survived without modern medicine.

I wondered how we were going to survive.

I should have come more prepared. Like Sophia had. I could have... brought...

I could have brought so many things.

And that, I realized was the answer. I had quite simply stumbled over it.

It had been there all along, but I just hadn't seen it.

I went to the window and looked outside. There was a storm gathering.

It was a good day for a storm.

"I need to run upstairs for a minute," I said. "I'll be right back."

"Okay," Mackenzie said, dropping into the chair I'd just vacated.

Kit Kat sat lifted his head, yawned and after looking around a moment, jumped into her lap.

I'd brought Kit Kat with me. Sophia had brought her Kindle and some medications.

I knew what I had to do.

46

GRANT

This was a hurricane. I was sure of it.

Four of us, Nathan, Andrew, Uncle Samuel, and me, all wielded hammers as we tacked the shutters closed over the windows.

Everyone was here, except for Cameron and Isabella. They had gone back to town yesterday. Cameron had a deadline on his novel and had to put it in the mail before he started on the next one.

The storm was coming in fast and hard.

It would be a lot less severe up here than it would have been if we were down south, but the wind could still do a lot of damage and there was the possibility of tornadoes.

It looked like it was going to hit us in the dead of night. The worst possible time—as though there was a good time—to be assaulted by a storm.

By the time we got all the windows secured, it was late afternoon and the rain was coming down.

We went in through the back door, already soaked.

Villars was there with blankets and hot coffee.

By the time we got dried off and warmed up, the storm was full on over our heads.

I needed sleep. We all needed sleep.

Between taking shifts sitting with Father and boarding up the windows, we were exhausted.

But we couldn't sleep. The women had gone up to bed, but we set up positions around the house to watch for damage.

If there was damage to part of the house, we needed to know it as soon as possible so we could do something about it.

It wouldn't do to wake up in the morning with half the house blown away.

I took my spot at the back of the house. Keeping watch out the back door. I paced from there to the kitchen and back again with nothing more than a meager candle to keep me company.

It would have been good if Cameron could have stayed around. We could have used another set of hands. But yesterday, the weather was just fine. No indications of a storm headed this way at all.

Victoria hadn't told me a lot about the future, but she had told me that people had gotten pretty good at predicting the weather. She'd even shown me a picture on the Kindle of what a hurricane looked like when it was brewing in the gulf.

Fascinating and frightening at the same time.

Sometimes, I believed, it was best to not know some things.

I poured some cold coffee into a cup and sipped it, mostly to give myself something to do.

There was one thing I had missed tonight.

I had missed telling Victoria good night.

But even more, I missed our good night kiss.

I worried that we weren't courting properly, and even told her so, but she didn't seem to be worried about it.

She'd just smiled and said we were doing just fine.

47

VICTORIA

This was not just a regular storm. The wind howled around the house, knocking limbs and debris against the covered windows.

Though I had no way to confirm it, it seemed more like a hurricane to me. I could tell by the way the clouds banked in little rows.

I'd even checked one of the weather history books on the Kindle for any record of a hurricane this year, but the records of that particular book didn't go back this far. This was probably even before people starting keeping records of such things.

They probably just wrote it off as another bad storm.

At any rate, it was good timing, all in all.

I stood in the foyer, watching the steady ticking of the grandfather clock and listening to the storm overhead.

There was something I hadn't told anyone.

I had the key.

I had the key to the clock. The one that was needed to use the formula for going through time.

I'd hidden it away in my room and all but forgotten about it.

But then it had occurred to me that I could use it. Now.

I had it figured out.

It was simple really.

I'd go back to the future. Get some high-powered antibiotics and whatever else I needed, then bring it all back.

I could write the prescription to myself, so I wouldn't have any problem getting what I needed.

The only thing that would hold me back was waiting for the next storm to happen.

My little scheme held some risk. No doubt about that.

It was possible that, since time was not linear, that I could get what I needed, then make it back here after it was too late to help Mr. Laurent.

I rationalized it though. If not Mr. Laurent, there would be someone else who needed medicine. Someone always needed medicine.

The men had come back inside after boarding up the windows and they had taken up watch around various points around the house.

That was quite smart of them. I wasn't sure I would have thought to do it.

I'd almost told Mackenzie what I was planning to do.

But I hadn't.

I had been afraid she would try to stop me.

She believed so hard in the whole soul mate concept.

She wasn't going to leave Andrew.

But I had to leave Grant

It was my fault Mr. Laurent was in the shape he was in.

Doc White would have given him quinine if I'd left him alone. Mr. Laurent would have survived the stuffy room.

He was not going to survive without medicine of some sort.

So I had to get it for him.

I had to make this right.

There was just enough light at the top of the landing window to let the lightning through.

I opened the glass and slid the key into the keyhole. Then just waited, biding my time.

The sooner I got this done, the sooner I could get what I needed from town and get back here.

Assuming there was a storm anytime soon in the future.

But since I couldn't control that, I chose not to worry about it.

When the lightning struck, with trembling fingers, I carefully turned the hands back one hour.

Then everything was quiet.

I didn't hear the thunder that followed. The storm was no longer howling outside.

I'd done it.

I stood very still and waited. Listening.

The first sound that registered was the roar of the air conditioning.

My hand shook as I closed the glass on the door of the clock face.

Then I swayed, leaning against the clock.

Things had not gone as planned after all.

I slowly dropped to my knees.

I had left the key in the past.

Without the key, I was stuck here.

With no way to return to the past.

48

GRANT

The old house had weathered the storm like a champion. As the wind died down, I'd fallen asleep with my head down on the kitchen table.

I'd just needed a little nap. Something to get me through.

"There's my venerable brother," Andrew said, coming into the kitchen with Mackenzie in tow.

Lifting my head, I scowled at him. "How is it you look so chipper this morning after staying up all night?"

"What makes you think he stayed up all night?" Mackenzie asked, sitting across from me and picking up a coffee cup. I hadn't seen anyone bring in the coffee pot and platter of fruit. Apparently I had been out cold.

"I guess I'm the only responsible one," I said as Mackenzie slid a cup of hot coffee across the table toward me.

"I guess," she said. "That must be difficult for you."

I scowled at her, but Andrew just grinned. "Try being married to a psychologist," he said.

I made a noncommittal sound in response.

"How's Father?" I asked.

"No change," Andrew said, sliding into the chair next to his wife.

"I guess I was hoping for a miracle."

"Has anyone seen Miss Victoria?" Villars asked, appearing at the door.

A shot of alarm shot through me.

"She's in her room," I said.

"No Sir," Villars said. "Mrs. Laurent sent for her, but she isn't there. Missus Sophia looked herself.

The wooden kitchen chair fell back against the floor as I shot out of it and headed out of the kitchen. I dashed past the foyer and took the stairs two at a time.

Going straight to Victoria's door, I didn't even have to worry about knocking. Her door stood wide open, Sophia and Nathan standing there, their heads bent close together.

They looked up when I stopped in front of them.

"Where is she?" I asked.

"We don't know," Nathan said.

Mackenzie and Andrew were behind me now.

"I might know," Mackenzie said and we all turned to look at her.

My heart was pounding dangerously fast. I dreaded her words because I knew what she was going to say before she even said.

"I think she may have gone to the future."

"Why?" Sophia asked, with a glance at me. "She's happy here."

"Yes," Mackenzie said. "but she feels responsible for Mr. Laurent."

"I talked to her about this," I said. "She is not responsible."

"She believes that Doc White would have given him quinine if she'd left him alone."

"Yeah," I scoffed. "That damn quack was also about to bleed him out with leeches. If anything, Victoria saved his life."

49

VICTORIA

I laid on the floor in the foyer for what could have been hours. Probably not that long, but I truly had no idea.

Finally, I dragged myself to my feet and put both hands against the silent grandfather clock. If this were a museum, I would be told not to touch it because it was so old.

But this wasn't a museum. This was my grandfather's home. And it was somehow a portal into the past.

A portal I had just screwed up.

Mr. Laurent needed my help and I couldn't help him.

I needed to think.

I went into the kitchen and turned on Grandpa's computer to check the date.

According to the computer I'd only been gone into the past for two days. So that meant Grandpa was still in rehab.

I took a bottle of water from the refrigerator and twisted off the lid. The water was cold and clean.

Taking a legal pad and pen, I sat at the kitchen table. Sometimes writing things down helped me to organize my thoughts. I was hoping it would help me now.

In this case, though, I wasn't sure where to start.

I started with my original plan.

Pick up medicine.

Return to the past.

It had seemed so simple in my head.

But now what was I supposed to do.

Pick up medicine.

Get it to the past.

But how? Without the key, I had no way to get things to the past. My sisters could send me messages, but I couldn't send them messages back.

With sudden inspiration, I ran upstairs to the guest room and grabbed the pry bar from the closet.

I sat on the floor in front of the window, my skirts spilling around me, and gently pried up the window frame.

My heart pounded as a letter spilled out. I unfold it with trembling hands.

But it was only the letter my sisters and I had left for Grandpa.

We're all here. Safely in 1854.

Victoria just got here. And she brought Kit Kat with her.

Victoria has a beau.

I dropped the letter in my lap.

Had a beau.

Well not anymore.

I wasn't going to win. Not either way.

It seemed the more I tried to help Grant's father, the more harm I did.

Well, at least being here I couldn't do any more harm.

Unfortunately, sitting idle was not in my nature. I sat there for all of about five minutes before I began to form a new plan.

It might not work, but at this point, I had nothing to lose.

50

GRANT

The rest of the day flew past. Sophia and Nathan went home to check their own house for damages.

Andrew went out to check his house, but Mackenzie, plagued with morning sickness, stayed behind.

After I told her about the notes Victoria and I had taken, we went into the library and began to look for answers.

Sophia had taken her Kindle with her. She was understandably very protective of it, but I had written down everything Victoria had said.

I handed Mackenzie the journal and paced back and forth while she read through my notes.

The clock chimed the hour, reminding me of Victoria and the time that separated us. Eleven chimes. Almost Noon.

"There's a willow tree out back," Mackenzie said.

"How do you know?" I asked, looking blankly at her.

"I asked Andrew," she said, with a shrug. "It looked different from the other trees, so I was curious."

"How did he know?"

"Andrew knows more than people give him credit for," she

said. "I've heard of willow bark tea," she said. "It's supposed to be medicinal. For fever, I think."

"Fever," I said. "You may have just found the answer."

"Victoria did," she said.

For the first time in days, I felt a glimmer of hope.

"I'll get a knife," I said.

"What do we do?" she asked, following me from the library. "Boil it?"

"We'll ask Villars," I said. "He'll know."

I took a knife from the kitchen and we headed down the path toward her house. The ground was muddy from last night's storm and we had to make our way carefully to avoid stepping in mud puddles.

She knew right where to find the willow tree.

I slowly peeled bark from the tree and placed it in the basket Mackenzie had brought.

"Is Victoria your soul mate?" she asked, startling me. I nearly cut myself with the knife.

I started to say *maybe* or to say I didn't know, but caught myself. Those answers would have been lies.

I knew perfectly well that Victoria was my soul mate.

"Yes," I said, finding a small branch and breaking it off. I could take my time later and whittle off the bark.

She grinned and adjusted the strips of bark in the basket.

"That's good," she said.

"Yeah?" I carefully slid my knife beneath the bark.

"Yes," she said. "Otherwise why would she have come here?"

"Do you ever wonder?" I asked. "why the four of you were born in the wrong century?"

She lifted a delicate eyebrow and looked at me with an expression that reminded me of Victoria.

"Perhaps we aren't the ones who were born in the wrong century," she said. "Besides maybe we had to learn what we did in our century in order to bring that knowledge back to you all."

I just looked at her as I put the knife up.

Damn. But she might be right.

51

VICTORIA

Three Weeks 4 Days Later

I had to give myself credit. I'd stayed three weeks after Grandpa came home from the hospital.

Three weeks longer than I would have bet anyone that I would have stayed.

Grandpa had a physical therapist coming out five days a week, plus he had Tracie full-time six days a week. Pretty soon he'd be doing laps around the house.

I had to get back to work after being idle three weeks longer than I had planned.

My bags were already in the car.

Grandpa has a doctor's appointment in Alexandria today, so the three of us, me, Tracie, and Grandpa were driving together. They'd drop me off at the airport, then Tracie would take Grandpa to the doctor.

It was an efficient trip.

I was up early, so I put on my running shoes, stretchy running pants, and tank top over a running bra. After pulling my hair back into a quick ponytail, I headed out the back door.

I ran the half mile to the highway, one mile along the river, then circled back. This would give me a good three-mile run.

A fog still hovered over the river water and I could barely see the water at all, much less the other side, nearly a mile away. The eerie sound

I crossed the highway and started back down the long dirt driveway leading to the house.

Tendrils of mist covered the ground making it hard for me to see the ground at my feet and the wind whipped at the long gray moss clinging to the tree limbs. I slowed my pace, to a slow jog.

There had been no rain in the forecast, but there were most definitely dark clouds brewing in the south.

A gust of wind whipped a strand of hair loose from my ponytail and I shoved it out of my face.

As I slowed, my heart rate accelerated. I'd been out in the mist like this before. Fifteen years ago.

I should have been able to see the house ahead of me, but too much fog had rolled in ahead of the storm.

I came to a stop. That's when I saw him.

Grant.

Standing there in front of me.

I thought I imagined him at first.

But his gaze locked onto mine and he walked toward me, covering the distance between us.

He stopped about three feet in front of me, the mist swirling around us.

But I saw him clearly. The soft end of the day stubble across his cheeks.

Strong. With chiseled features.

I knew those eyes. Those lips.

This mist swirled around us, seeming to pull us closer together.

He held out his arms and I stepped into them.

52

GRANT

I had gone for a walk to clear my head.

It had taken a week, but the willow bark tea had worked. Father was sitting up now, eating some eggs that Villars had brought to his room.

Things could go back to normal now. Father had survived.

The mist had rolled in shortly after I left the house.

I'd almost turned around. Returned to the house, but something compelled me to keep moving forward. I could do nothing else.

I'd walked along the dirt driveway leading to the main river road.

And now Victoria was in my arms.

The wasn't my imagination. She was real.

I pulled back and cupped her cheeks with my hands, looking into her eyes.

"You're here," I murmured.

"Yes."

"How?"

"I don't know.

I pressed my lips against hers.

It didn't matter how.

It only mattered that she was here.

"You'll stay?" I asked.

She nodded.

I kissed her again, pulling her hair loose from the band that held it back in the process.

Then she pulled back, distress in her expression.

"Your father?" she asked.

"He's better," I said. "On the way to recovery."

"But how?"

"You figured it out," I said. "The willow bark tea."

"It worked?"

"Yes."

She dropped her head against my chest. "Thank God," she breathed. "I thought..."

I wrapped my arms around her and held her close.

It was time to go home. For me to take her home.

I bent down and picked her up and she wrapped her arms around my neck.

"How long was I gone?" she asked.

"A week," I said. "but it felt like an eternity."

"I didn't think I'd be able to come back. Not without the key."

"The key?" I looked blankly at her. "You had the key?"

"I did. I mean I had it here. It's still here. But I couldn't get back here without it."

"It takes more than a missing key to keep us apart," I said. I stopped. "Make me a promise," I said.

"Okay."

"Promise me you'll never leave me again."

"Don't worry," she said. "I won't."

I kissed her again.

"We've been here before," I said against her lips.

She nodded.
"Fifteen years ago."
"You did remember."
"Of course I did," she said.
"But this time it's forever."

EPILOGUE

VICTORIA

Three Weeks Later

Emma was gone again, so Mackenzie played the piano. As always, she played like an angel. She could have easily pursued music, but she was good at psychology, too.

It was one of those lovely summer evenings, a balmy breeze coming in through the open windows.

Everyone was here. My two sisters and even my brother and Isabella had come in from town for the weekend.

Mr. Laurent sat with his wife on one side of the room.

I sat with Grant, snuggled against him.

The ring on my finger had belonged to his mother's mother. It hadn't mattered to Mrs. Laurent that her two youngest sons and her daughter had married first, she'd saved this ring for her oldest son.

Everyone seemed to think that I had saved Mr. Laurent's life. I didn't think so, but there no point in arguing.

Things had happened to get us all here to this moment. I would never again question the power of fate.

Or destiny.

I'd been destined to be with Grant from the very beginning. I knew that deep within my soul.

I'd known it since that day when I'd been fifteen. The day I'd met Grant in the mist.

He brought our linked hands to his lips and kissed the backs of my fingers.

"Are you happy?" he asked.

"I couldn't be happier."

"It's our wedding day," he said. "Are you sure there's nothing else you need?"

"I have everything I need right here," I said, leaning my cheek against his chest.

"We'll send your Grandpa a letter tomorrow letting him know that you're here. That we're married."

"Okay," I said. "But he knows. I'm sure he knows."

Grandpa had watched so many people he loved leave him to go back in time. I couldn't imagine how hard that must have been for him. I hated it that he didn't have the capability to travel through time. He'd never said, but I had a feeling he would if he could.

As the grandfather clock began to chime the hour, I gazed into Grant's beautiful blue eyes.

After the ninth and final chime hung in the air, I looked over at Mackenzie. She smiled at me across the room.

Grant kissed me on the cheek and I looked back at him.

"It's getting late," he said. "maybe we should head upstairs."

"Yes," I said. "Maybe we should."

He stood up and pulled me to my feet, my dress flowing around me.

No one seemed to notice as we slipped from the room and went upstairs.

I didn't know what life held from here.

It didn't matter. Whatever it was, it would be here. With Grant.

In this time.

And that was all I could ask for.

Keep Reading for a Preview of
TRAPPED IN THE MELODY…

TRAPPED IN THE MELODY PREVIEW

Prologue
Emma Becquerel
November 1855

My fingers slid easily over the smooth piano keys, the strains of what was supposed to be a joyful melody filling the evening air.

I winced as I hit a wrong note, throwing off the whole piece. As long as I looked at the music, I could play okay, but Mother insisted that I practice playing by memory.

Even now, mother sat across the room next to the warmth of the fireplace, working her needlepoint. I shivered. It hardly seemed fair. I, too, wanted to sit in front of the warm fire and read.

Shivering, even with a shawl draped around my shoulders, I wore a long-sleeved light blue wool dress with a full skirt that belled out around me when I stood up. Not like a ball gown, but a normal day dress.

I didn't particularly like playing the piano. Not really. I wouldn't mind being a pianist, but since I wasn't willing to put in the countless hours of practice, I would never get to that professional level where I could entertain guests with my skills. So even though I knew it and Mother knew it, she would never admit that I was wasting my time playing every evening.

I would much prefer to work at my sketches or to sit and read. Either one would be far more enjoyable to me. I found much more meaning in those things than I did learning an instrument whose sole purpose was to impress and entertain others.

The grandfather clock standing in the foyer chimed the hour telling me I had only thirty minutes left to play before I could be excused.

The clock's chimes joined in with the piano's melody, softening the notes of the song I played.

Now that I was seventeen, old enough for a husband, I could be married soon and be out from beneath my mother's iron thumb.

Although I had been reluctant to accept the idea, I was beginning to think that maybe it was time.

My fingers still on the keys, I looked to my right, toward the shadowy foyer.

And that's when I saw him.

A tall, lean young man standing at the door watching me play. He wore a short dark coat and an odd-looking cap.

I missed a few notes, then just started playing the one song I knew from memory, so I wouldn't have to look back at the music.

A quick glance in Mother's direction told me didn't notice the change in melody, nor did she see the man. She hadn't even looked up from her needlepoint.

Perhaps the man was one of Father's guests. It was odd,

though, because the stranger appeared to be alone. No one was with him. Not Father. Not the butler.

I wondered if I should be alarmed, but he didn't look dangerous.

As my song ended, Mother looked up at me with that look that insisted I keep playing.

So I did and even though I kept my eyes on the sheet music, I had trouble keeping my place. It was most disconcerting with the stranger watching me like this.

I stole a glance toward him. He stood at the doorway, leaning against the doorframe, watching me. He was young. My age. And very handsome.

My fingers stumbled.

Unable to play any longer, I lifted my fingers from the keys. I closed my eyes and counted to ten.

"I'm sorry, Mother," I said. "I'm not feeling well. I have to stop."

Mother just shrugged.

"Very well," she said. "You can be excused."

I cautiously raised my gaze to the foyer, but the man was no longer there.

I hadn't seen him leave. I watched the foyer a moment, but he didn't come back.

Perhaps I had imagined him.

I straightened the piano music and put it away, tucking it beneath the bench seat for tomorrow when it would be there to torture me again.

I headed out of the parlor before Mother changed her mind.

As I crossed through the doorway into the foyer, I could smell the man who had just been standing there.

A deep woodsy scent with undertones of lavender.

It woke all my feminine sensibilities.

Yes. It was time for me to think about taking a husband.

Chapter 1
James Boucheron
Present Day

To say that I was down on my luck was an understatement.

Stabbing the shovel deep into the soft earth, I dug up a dried out dead plant, roots and all, and tossed it into the wheelbarrow.

I had to stop and pull off my flannel shirt, tossing it aside. Between the warmth of the morning sun and the warmth radiating from the pile of leaves and debris behind me, I was no longer cold.

I dumped my collection of debris from the wheelbarrow onto the fire and used a rake to keep the flames from spreading. Little sparks flew high into the sky, hopefully cooling off before they landed in one of the huge oak trees overhead. The leaves were falling off the limbs, but the moss didn't appear to be affected by the cold November weather.

The house behind me was a large four-story Greek style house with large white columns lining the veranda. The wooden columns, painted white, had withstood the centuries surprisingly well. But the house, built in the early 1800s, badly needed a coat of paint. Maybe I would get to that next.

I'd been here to the Becquerel Estate once before when I was a teen. My father had come here on business with Jonathan Becquerel and I'd come with him.

We'd only been here for one night, but the place had left a lasting impression on me.

Other than that, I couldn't explain why I had been drawn to this place when I lost everything.

We had been wealthy. Billionaires. But for two years, one

wrong turn after another had steadily pulled us down. Then my father's death had put a nail in not only his coffin, but that of any wealth the family had as well.

I had left Atlanta as a debtor.

Though I had not thought it was possible, I found myself literally on the streets with nothing but the clothes on my back.

One night in the homeless shelter had been one night too many.

I'd left the next morning, hitchhiking my way to Natchez. It had taken me three days.

From there, I had set off walking toward the Becquerel Estate. Between walking and riding on the back of someone's pickup truck, I'd made it here from town in two hours.

Jonathan Becquerel, the owner of this old place, was older now, moving slowly, and had a caregiver named Tracie who lived with him.

Tracie hadn't liked it when Jonathan had taken me in and after a long conversation he'd agreed to give me a place to stay in exchange for helping him out around here.

God knows he needed the help.

Tracie stayed busy inside, doing a decent job of keeping things up, though most of her time was spent caring for Jonathan. Needless to say, the outside of the house had been neglected.

I wasn't a gardener, by any means, but I was good with my hands and I was a quick learner.

My parents had given us chores—indoor and outdoor—when we were growing up, so I was somewhat acquainted with manual labor. Fortunately Jonathan had gloves I could wear.

This mindless work gave me time to think.

I needed to come up with a plan.

My father may have left me penniless, but I had skills. I had a master's degree in finance and had worked for my father. I knew the markets.

The problem was, however, that I was flat out broke.

I would come up with a way out of this mess.

I didn't know the solution was yet, but I'd come up with something.

My gaze was drawn toward the house again.

I'd never forgotten what I had seen that night I'd stayed here with my father.

The vision of the most beautiful girl I'd ever seen sitting at the piano had haunted me over the last fifteen years. She'd had long blonde hair framing a heart shape face. Large dark eyes and lush lips curled into a sexy little pout.

I could still see her clearly. I could hear the hear the badly played music.

The odd thing was that neither Jonathan nor my father had seen her nor had they heard the music.

And they had been standing right next to me.

Chapter 2
Emma
November 1858

THREE YEARS HAD PASSED SINCE THAT NIGHT I'D SEEN THE MAN standing in the foyer.

And for three years he'd haunted my dreams.

And despite my decision—one I had made that very night—to choose a husband, I'd compared every eligible bachelor who came within my path to him.

A man I had not even met. I had not seen him up close. I didn't know his name. No one else had even seen him.

Apparently, Father had not had any guest that night.

So even though I believed I had invented the man—I even

referred to him as "The Man" in my thoughts—he was the one I compared all others to.

"Where is your dance card?" Mother asked as we walked together toward the stairs.

It was the annual Becquerel Autumn Ball and everyone who was anyone would be in attendance. That meant there would be countless eligible bachelors in need of a wife. Whether or not they knew they needed a wife was another matter entirely.

"It's right here," I said, lifting the dreaded dance card strapped to my wrist. After countless balls and barbeques, I knew that there would be no one who here who matched the image I carried in my head.

Already the music from the orchestra drifted upstairs and people were making their way in through the front door.

The French doors would be open to allow cool air inside and to allow guests to spill outside, provided the weather didn't get too cold.

Carriages were lined up along the oak tree canopied lane, each family eagerly waiting their turn to come inside and join the festivities.

Everyone knew that my brother, Martin, was home from West Point, so whether Mother wanted to admit it or not, he was the main attraction at tonight's ball.

I didn't mind. It actually should have taken some of the pressure off me and it would have except that Mother wore her sternest expression as we made our way downstairs.

"Make sure you fill every dance," she said.

"Of course, Mother," I said, sighing to myself.

It was going to be a long night.

Unless there was someone new at tonight's ball... a marriageable gentleman I had yet to meet, I would be beleaguered by the same men I'd been dancing with for the past two to three years.

Handsy. Dull. Self-absorbed.

I had honestly grown somewhat disheartened that the handsome mystery man would show up again provided, of course, that I had not invented him in my own head.

Perhaps tonight things would change.

Fortunately, other than Mother, most people would be focused on my brother and not me.

Perhaps I'd be able to slip off to the library and avoid dancing with the most wearisome suitors.

As we neared the first floor, the clock began to chime.

Six chimes.

And off we went.

Chapter 3
James

THE BEST THING ABOUT WORKING FOR JONATHAN BECQUEREL was that he allowed me to freely roam his home.

Although I didn't really know how he could possibly remember me, I hoped for his sake that he did.

Letting a total stranger into his home was dangerous and Tracie had every right to be cautious.

Three days had passed and still, she looked at me with suspicion whenever our paths crossed. Smart girl.

Except in this case, I'd been honest and I was harmless.

At any rate, the best part of being here, besides having a safe, comfortable place to stay, was having access to his computer and Internet. Since I didn't have so much as a cell phone at the moment, I would have otherwise been completely out of touch with the world.

I watched YouTube videos and took countless notes, hoping for some inspiration as to how to essentially start over.

Alone.

My father had done it. His parents had brought him here from France and he had started with nothing.

I could do it, too.

But Father had taken us down hard.

And that was going to be even harder to come back from.

My name, for those who recognized it, was tainted with failure.

I considered changing my name and held that in reserve for a last resort.

We were still a good family. My father's financial failures shouldn't change that.

Shouldn't was always a key word.

I barely noticed when the rain started, coming down outside the window behind me, but when lightning struck near me, I was reminded that I was in the country.

I was even more reminded ten minutes later when the electricity went out.

I'd moved over to the armchair, bringing the laptop computer with me.

The only light in the room came from that computer.

The Internet was fried. No service.

That must have been some lightning strike. My ears were ringing and I couldn't hear a thing.

I slowly closed the lid and set the computer on the table next to me.

Had there been a table there earlier? I couldn't remember.

I stood up, then I heard the music.

Not music from a television or a radio.

Not piano music like I'd heard that night fifteen years ago.

But orchestra music. And live orchestra music if I remembered anything from life before.

I crossed to the door and stopped.

There was a party on the other side of that door. I'd stake my life on it.

And considering that my life was really all I had left, that was saying something.

I opened the door and poked my head out.

A tall, debonair, and distinguished man walked in my direction. He carried himself as a butler would.

"Good evening," he said, stopping two feet in front of me. "Can I be of assistance?"

"I'm a little confused," I said.

"My name is Villars. I'm the butler." His gaze swept over me, almost imperceptibly.

"I need to see Jonathan," I said.

"Jonathan," the man said. "Right." Then he leaned forward. "Might I make a suggestion?"

"Of course," I said. The man reminded me of the butler I'd grown up with. His name had been Edgar and he'd always been present in our household the whole time I'd lived at home.

Sadly enough, I didn't even know what had become of Edgar.

"If you'll wait here," he said. "I'll bring you something appropriate to wear."

I smiled. And just like Edgar, Villars was here to look out for us.

Keep Reading Trapped in the Melody…

Kathryn Kaleigh is the author of sixty-eight novels, over one hundred short stories, and many collections.

kathrynkaleigh.com

www.ingramcontent.com/pod-product-compliance
Lightning Source LLC
Chambersburg PA
CBHW030337310726
48979CB00001B/78

* 9 7 8 1 6 4 7 9 1 3 9 5 3 *